NO VIRGIN ISLAND

A Sabrina Salter Mystery

C. Michele Dorsey

CROOKED
LANE

NEW YORK

Copyright © 2015 by C. Michele Dorsey

All rights reserved.

Published in the United States by Crooked Lane Books, an imprint of The Quick Brown Fox & Company LLC.

Crooked Lane Books and its logo are trademarks of The Quick Brown Fox & Company LLC.

The Library of Congress Cataloging-in-Publication Data is available upon request.

ISBN (hardcover): 978-1-62953-190-8
e-ISBN: 978-1-62953-203-5

Cover design by Lori Palmer
Book design by Jennifer Canzone

Printed in the United States.

www.crookedlanebooks.com

Crooked Lane Books
2 Park Avenue, 10th Floor
New York, NY 10016

First Edition: August 2015

10 9 8 7 6 5 4 3 2 1

For Steve,
The best is yet to be . . .

Chapter One

Sabrina Salter was a woman who didn't like surprises, even nice ones. Surprises were setups at best and almost always meant to benefit the donor. That was why the sight of the villa guest's rental jeep, still parked in the driveway, made Sabrina's stomach clench.

He should have been long gone. Checkout was at 10:00 a.m. That was the rule. It was already 10:35. But why should she expect him to follow the rules? St. John was a magnet for rule breakers, including her.

She pulled her ridiculous gecko-green-colored jeep behind his black-forest-green model, the color Sabrina had wanted to buy for the business, and decided not to bring in her cleaning bucket just yet. She got out, noticing that at least his duffle bag was in his backseat. But there was no sight of the large camera bag or backpack he'd had with him when she had picked him up on arrival. Maybe he was getting a couple of last shots.

She hesitated for a moment but then approached the gate to Villa Mascarpone, bracing for a fight she didn't want to have. Sabrina hated conflict. But she had new guests arriving later that afternoon and plenty to do to get the house ready for them.

"Inside," she called, using the island greeting to let him know she was entering.

No response. She tried again. Nothing. She pressed the latch to the periwinkle blue gate and pushed it open.

Sabrina knew the man in the hammock was dead because she knew what dead looked like. The bull's-eye red stain in the middle of his Skinny Legs Bar and Grill T-shirt was a giveaway, not to mention the insects swirling around his sagging body. He was lying crooked, his sunglasses half slung off his eyes, as if he had been blasted by force back onto the hammock. He looked nothing like the rugged, handsome, bearded man who had booked an entire villa just for himself at the last minute.

Sabrina felt her spine arch as she looked to the left of the pool area where the hammock hung between two pillars that were part of a pergola, designed to offer shade from the blast of heat the tropical sun delivered each day. Seagulls and frigatebirds hovered above the pergola, which protected the corpse like an open-air mausoleum. Standing just inside the gate to the pool area, her flip-flops glued to the tile, Sabrina looked over to the other side of the pool, where the villa's sliding glass doors were locked with a padlock, just as she instructed all guests to do upon departure. She doubted anyone was in the house because it was built into a steep cliff, as most houses in St. John were, and the only entrance was through the sliders. There was no escape down the side of the cliff, where only goats could navigate the vertical slopes. The sole sound came from the surf crashing below.

Sabrina refused to move any closer to the body. He was dead and there was nothing she could do for him, poor soul. Her only contact with the local police since she had moved to St. John had left her reluctant to do anything that might antagonize them.

In the sliver of an instant, Sabrina knew her life had changed forever, simply because she had the bad luck to find the dead body of a murder victim. This was so incredibly unfair. She had just begun to feel like she had a life in St. John and was beginning to make friends, which she hadn't dreamed possible after Nantucket. She'd even been invited to join a book club and had actually accepted the invitation. Now that was all slipping away along with the spirit of the dead man on the hammock.

Sabrina knew she should call the police immediately, but the thought of dialing 911 frightened her more than the idea that the killer might still be present, which she doubted. She knew one short telephone call would end the new life she had struggled so hard to create. It wasn't a lavish life; why couldn't she just be left alone? All she had wanted to do was to clean Villa Mascarpone, one of ten villas she managed on the smallest of the three U.S. Virgin Islands.

Her partner, Henry Whitman, had implored her, as only Henry could implore, to take this villa cleanup from his schedule because he'd happened to "get lucky" with a hot date that he was certain would last through this morning. Even though she had nothing to do with the death of the villa guest, the cops would want to connect her to this mess. They hated her being on their island. But she knew that she had no choice—that if she left and waited for someone else to discover the body and the police found out, it would look even worse. She dialed 911 from her cell phone, which the gods of the Caribbean had deigned to provide her with reception, for once. A dispatcher named Lucy Detree informed her the call was being recorded.

"I'm up at Villa Mascarpone in Fish Bay," Sabrina said.

"What do you want, ma'am?" the female dispatcher asked, sounding bored by the call. Sabrina hated being called "ma'am."

"I've found a dead body. He's lying in a hammock. He's got blood on his shirt," she said.

"Are you sure he's dead?" Detree interrupted.

Was she sure? He looked as dead as her late husband had the night a bullet had blasted through his belly.

"I'm pretty sure. Do you want me to get closer to check? I know you guys don't like people getting too close to the scene of a crime," she added, desperate not to irritate the cops. She still wanted to be the good girl, the one who played by the rules and didn't upset people, even though it had never really worked. Whether she aimed for perfect or invisible, she still managed to be in the way.

"Why do you think he's dead?" the dispatcher asked.

Sabrina described the amount of blood and the insects and mentioned that a couple of seagulls and frigates had begun swirling above the man.

"Okay, he sounds dead. What's your name?"

"Sabrina Salter." Silence lingered in the air.

"You stay there. Do not leave the scene. Do not touch anything, anything at all. You understand me, Ms. Salter? I have my men on their way, you get this?"

"Yes, yes, I follow you," Sabrina said, looking over at the gulls laughing at the prospect of lunch in a hammock and wishing she could just turn the clock back and pretend this wasn't happening.

"You got a lawyer on island, Ms. Salter? You might want to give him a head's up," Officer Detree said.

Instead, Sabrina called her partner. Henry was the one man on the planet Sabrina trusted. They had met during Sabrina's frequent flights from Boston to New York, when she was working as a television meteorologist and Henry was working first class as a flight attendant for Allied Air. Henry would tease Sabrina about forecasters never getting it right. Slowly, after countless conversations during flights, they became friends. When Sabrina's world fell apart, Henry called her to offer support. He had been the only one. Sabrina reciprocated when Henry had to resign from Allied Air after a scandal that nearly destroyed him.

She remembered she was not the only person who came to St. John to escape and hated telling him there had been a murder at one of the villas they managed.

"Why are you calling me? You said you'd cover," Henry said, mumbling into the speaker, which Sabrina pictured lying on a pillow, barely aimed at his pouting mouth.

"Yeah, I said I'd cover for you and clean this place for the next set of guests coming this afternoon. I didn't say I'd cover for you and discover the last guest had been murdered here," Sabrina said, feeling angry with Henry for something she knew wasn't his fault. She didn't care. This wasn't her fault either, but she knew it wouldn't matter after the cops and the media were done with her. They would have her all over tabloid television again.

"Murdered?" Henry said, now sounding alert.

"Henry, get up here quick. Please, the cops are on their way. I don't want to be here with them on my own."

"I'm on my way, honey. Don't let them bully you if they beat me there. Don't say anything." Sabrina could hear clothing rustling and him whispering good-bye to whatever lucky guy he'd been with.

"I won't," she said through the lump in her throat. "Thanks."

"Just tell me so I know what we're dealing with, sweetie. Did you do it?"

Chapter Two

Sabrina stood in the driveway of Villa Mascarpone. Even with the midday tropical sun beating down on her, she felt chilled and wished she had a hoodie in her jeep. "Don't touch anything." "Call your lawyer." The words of the dispatcher repeated in her ears, as if she had murdered the man, as if she'd done anything to him besides discover his body.

She heard the sound of Henry's motor scooter in the far distance rounding the sharp curves on the dirt road leading to the villa, which sat at the top of a bluff with two others. It was a dead end. You could go no farther on St. John from this point without a boat or a pair of wings. She looked over at the other two villas, saw no one, no cars, nothing.

She was terrified. Not of the dead man. Not even of the person who had killed him. Sabrina had grown to consider her life in two segments. There was Before Nantucket, when she'd scrambled from a hellish childhood into a modicum of success and normalcy. And there was After Nantucket, when she'd lost everything except her freedom. She was damned if she was going to let anyone threaten it now.

If there was anything good about her experience in Nantucket, it was that she had experience dealing with the police. She had a choice and needed to decide fast whether she would continue to play the good girl and sit on her hands while she waited for Henry and the cops or whether she should grab the next few minutes while no one was around and see for herself if there was anything the police would find that might complicate her life further. She didn't believe there was anything that might implicate her, but she wasn't sure what she might find. If she didn't act now, the opportunity would be lost forever. She needed to conduct the search before Henry arrived to witness it so he wouldn't be put in the position of having to lie to the cops about it.

Sabrina grabbed the vinyl gloves from her cleaning bucket out of her jeep and slipped them over her shaking hands. She walked over to the man's rental jeep and opened the door. She grabbed the duffle, placed it on the seat, and unzipped it, rummaging through shorts and T-shirts and what smelled like sweaty socks. She found nothing of interest, although she wasn't sure what she was looking for. She just knew she didn't need any more surprises in her life. The jeep was otherwise empty, with only a sprinkle of sand on the floor by the driver's seat. The guy hadn't spent much time at the beach, which was odd, considering all the fancy camera equipment he came with.

Where was the camera bag? Was it with the backpack, which was missing as well? Sabrina doubted he'd left them in the house, but she wasn't going to leave it to chance. She knew she had at least another five minutes before Henry or the cops arrived. While she was convinced the house was empty, the idea of confirming her theory was frightening. But more alarming was the thought that something inside the house could be used to pin the death of the man on her. She stepped through the gate once more, glancing over toward the sagging hammock weighted almost to the deck by the large man. Quickly confirming his backpack and camera bag weren't there, she walked over toward the sliding glass doors, leaving the gloves on. The police would expect to find her fingerprints in the house, but not on the bags, and if she found either one, she planned to search it.

Without realizing it, Sabrina began to play the familiar tape in her head, the mantra given to her forty years ago by Ruth, the woman who had raised her, when she was just a four-year-old: "I, Sabrina, am not afraid. I, Sabrina, am fearless." How many times had she whispered those words, spoken them inside her head, even occasionally shouting them?

Sabrina moved quickly through the four-bedroom villa, her eyes alert for anything out of order, while she silently chanted Ruth's gift to her. No sight of either bag.

The place had been left in decent shape, given it had been occupied for two weeks by a man on vacation. Satisfied that there was nothing obvious the police could use against her, Sabrina put the padlock back on the door and retreated through the gate, tossing her purple cleaning gloves back into the bucket. She checked the driveways of the other two villas for vehicles. Still none.

She leaned against her jeep, catching her breath. Other than the sound of waves crashing onto jagged rocks hundreds of feet below, there was absolute quiet in Fish Bay, where Villa Mascarpone was perched on a steep, unpaved road with no guardrail.

Sabrina turned at the sound of a motor approaching and saw a cloud of dust rising up from the road before Henry appeared. He looked immaculate in white cotton Bermuda shorts and a white Oxford cloth button down with the sleeves rolled up to show his tanned forearms. A stifled cry of relief escaped from the back of her throat as Henry got off his school-bus-yellow scooter like a knight dismounting his stallion.

Sabrina stood planted in front of the open gate, hoping to block the view of the body for Henry until she could first describe the scene.

"How can you look so fabulous in such short notice?" she asked, marveling at how impervious Henry was to dust. She had a talent for attracting both dirt and dirtbags.

"Easy, I picked this outfit off the chair. I wore it to Asolare last night." He gathered her in a big bear hug, which brought his eyes just above her shoulders where a full view of the hammock could be seen.

"Oh, dear Lord," Henry said, backing away from her embrace, the color of his face matching his outfit. Covering his mouth with one hand, he staggered toward the Plumbago hedge, which bordered the driveway, and retched into a Sago Palm.

"Are you okay?" Sabrina asked, watching Henry pull an ironed white hankie from his back pocket and dab at his lips.

"Well, I'm better than he is, that's for sure. Who would do something like this? Why? How will we ever clean that stain off the deck? That stone is absorbent as hell. And what about the people who are due to arrive here at three?" Henry asked.

"We'll have to switch them to another house," Sabrina said, realizing how complicated the untimely death of the houseguest, whose name she had blocked out, had made her day. She looked around at the blues and greens of the Caribbean surrounding Villa Mascarpone, the cloudless sky above, and the tropical blossoms bursting everywhere. This was supposed to be paradise. She had talked Henry into joining her in St. John and starting Ten Villas when his life fell apart not long after hers. St. John was a perfect place for a fresh start, she'd told him. And it had been, until now.

Sabrina heard the sound of multiple sirens in the distance, growing closer as Henry took several deep breaths. Three police cruisers arrived in tandem, doors flying open, six cops popping out, all with guns drawn.

"Don't shoot. We didn't do anything." Henry raised his hands in surrender.

"Where's the body?" asked a tall, solid officer dressed in a deep blue T-shirt with a U.S. Virgin Islands emblem on a chest pocket. He wore matching blue pants, which had gold stripes running down the outside of his tree-stump legs. He was the police version of business casual.

Sabrina nodded toward the open gate.

"Did you touch anything?" he asked.

"No, of course not," she said, insulted that he wasn't giving her credit for her experience with dead bodies. She understood proper police protocol.

The officer's name was Leon Janquar. Sabrina remembered him from the time there had been a burglary in one of their villas. During their brief conversation then, he'd told her that he knew about Nantucket. But today, he didn't seem to remember her. Or maybe he did and the head games had already begun.

Janquar instructed one of the younger officers to remain with Henry and her in the driveway, while the other five approached the gate and proceeded inside.

Within five minutes, Janquar returned to the driveway and radioed headquarters in Cruz Bay that the victim discovered in Fish Bay was indeed dead, having bled to death after suffering a gunshot wound to the upper abdomen. Sabrina heard him say they found no other person present on the grounds and that the windows and doors leading to decks above ground level were all locked. Janquar instructed whomever he was talking to on the radio to call St. Thomas to get the SOCO squad over to St. John.

Sabrina leaned over and whispered to Henry that they were calling for scene-of-the-crime officers.

"I know that. I watch CSI," Henry said.

"Okay, which of you found the body?" Janquar asked.

"I did," Sabrina said, making sure there was no hesitation in her voice. She remembered what they did to you if you didn't sound sure of yourself.

"And who are you?" asked Detective Janquar.

Relieved that he really didn't seem to remember her from the burglary at one of her vacation homes, Sabrina explained that she was the co-owner of Ten Villas and that Henry was her partner. Villa Mascarpone was one of the villas they managed and rented to vacationers.

"Did you rent this house to the victim?" Janquar asked.

"His name is Carter Johnson, Officer," Henry said. Sabrina was grateful he had spared her the embarrassment of not remembering the dead man's name.

"Do either of you have a key to that padlock on the sliders?" Janquar asked in a tone Sabrina found accusatory.

"We both do. We always carry keys to all of the homes we manage," Sabrina said.

"Well, I'm only interested in the key to this house, so hand it over."

Sabrina slid the key off the ring of house keys she wore attached to her belt next to her cell phone and a few small tools.

Janquar took the key off the ring and handed it to the two officers who had been watching the driveway.

"Make sure no one's in there. Keep your weapons out until you're certain," he told them.

"Oh, I'm pretty sure no one is in there. It looks like he locked up and then was killed," Sabrina said.

"You an expert in these matters, Mrs. Salter? I seem to remember you have a history with men killed on islands, don't you?"

Henry stepped forward to stand next to her on the driveway.

"That was different. She was fully exonerated in Nantucket, sir."

"And it's *Ms.* Salter," Sabrina said, knowing she might anger Janquar but no longer caring.

"So what do you know about this guy, *Miss* Salter?" Janquar asked, upping the ante.

"Only that he rented this house by himself for the past two weeks and that he was from New Jersey. And it's *Mizzz* Salter, Detective."

"How many times did you see him?"

"Just the day he arrived when I met him at the ferry, took him to pick up his jeep, and showed him the way out here and around the house."

"Pretty big house for one guy. Are you sure he was alone?" Janquar asked, pushing his sunglasses back up from where they had slid down his sweaty nose.

"As far as I know," Sabrina said. She could hear her voice becoming increasingly defensive and wondered when he would stop firing questions.

Henry chimed in. "Villa Mascarpone is one of our most popular villas. What with a view of St. Thomas and Puerto Rico from the back deck, St. Croix from the side porch, and Ram Head and Bordeaux Mountain over here, you have a perfect panorama, whether you are a party of one or of eight."

"Save it for the website," Janquar said.

"Do you have any more questions? Because we need to find alternative arrangements for the people who booked this house and are arriving on the three o'clock ferry." Sabrina sensed that it was time for Henry and her to shut up and get out before they said something really stupid. She heard a car pulling up behind the police vehicles and wondered if the SOCO team had arrived.

"Oh, I have plenty of questions for you, Mizzz Salter," Janquar said.

Sabrina heard the familiar voice of Neil Perry before she could see him.

"Well, they're going to have to wait, unless you're ready to charge my client with something. I imagine she's shattered at finding a body, and I'll need some time to speak with her alone before this interview continues."

Chapter Three

"Counsel," Janquar said, nodding at Neil, who managed to look distinguished in his flip-flops and Ray Bans. He was a tall, tan man wearing cut-offs and a T-shirt with the words "Bar None" written below the scales of justice, which were pictures of inverted martini glasses.

"Neil? How did you—" Sabrina began, but quickly turned to Henry. "Did you?" Henry was the only one who knew Sabrina found Neil attractive enough to tempt her to break her self-inflected ban on men in her life.

"Guilty as charged," Henry said, moving toward his scooter. "I'd best move on so that the Leonards will have a house tonight. Shall we tuck them in Tide-Away?" Henry asked while mounting his scooter.

"Sure. Maybe I should come help you," Sabrina said, although she knew Tide-Away was probably in decent shape and would require only minimal efforts after Henry's sleepover.

"Just say we're upgrading them at no extra charge when you pick them up at the ferry," said Henry.

"As long as Detective Janquar's done with you for the moment," Neil said, "you need to come to my office as—"

He was interrupted by the sound of a vehicle approaching. A navy-blue jeep came into view.

"Oh no. Do we have curiosity creeps already?" Janquar said, disgust rolling off his tongue. Sabrina knew what he meant by curiosity creeps. They were the people who considered a crime site a scenic view, a shrine to visit even years later. They were the ones who called in to talk shows, night after night, to ask questions about the crime, investigation, and trial, waiting hours on the line to get through. Worse were the authorities, the callers who scrutinized and weighed the forensic evidence, sharing their theories about why the accused was guilty and should go straight to hell.

"No, no," Sabrina said. "That's Lyla and Evan. They live over there," she said pointing at the house. Lyla and Evan Banks were an elderly couple who had recently moved from New York City to retire on St. John at the villa across the way from Villa Mascarpone.

Sabrina watched Lyla, always the one to drive, pull into her driveway. Within seconds, Lyla was out of the jeep staring at the busy officers who were now swarming the driveway and outer yard like navy-blue ants at a picnic. One was winding crime scene tape around the property line, cinching Villa Mascarpone at the waist.

Evan emerged from the passenger door and went to hoist a plastic bag from Starfish Market out of the backseat.

Sabrina heard him telling Lyla, "Why don't I just bring the frozen stuff in the house while you run over and see what it's all about, dear? I'll join you in a minute." Though the Alzheimer's was barely noticeable to anyone else, Sabrina knew Lyla felt crushed whenever the slightest sign of Evan's deterioration showed, and she guessed that before becoming ill, he would never have let Lyla approach a police scene alone. Sabrina was also reminded about the close proximity of the driveways of the three villas sitting at the top of the hill were and how easily you could hear conversations taking place in them.

"What's going on here? Whatever has happened? Are you all right, dear?" Lyla asked as she approached Neil, Janquar, and Sabrina but looked directly at Sabrina. "I thought we'd left this kind of thing behind us when we left New York."

Sabrina wanted to reach out and hug Lyla, which surprised her because she was not the hugging kind. Henry was always trying to give her a hug for this or that and she wanted no part of it. But Lyla Banks was her friend and seemed frightened.

When Lyla and Evan first moved to the neighborhood, Henry had introduced himself and let the Banks know that Ten Villas managed their neighbor, Villa Mascarpone. Lyla had invited Henry and her to dinner. Sabrina had insisted to Henry she didn't want to go, didn't want to get involved with people, especially not old people. But Henry had been adamant. If they were going to make their business work, they had to become part of the small island community. "No man is an island," he said, before she agreed just to shut him up.

Not long after she and Henry had arrived for dinner, Evan, tall, lean, and charming, a retired math professor, had bragged to them how brave Lyla was because she was making a new recipe for them, a seafood casserole, which Sabrina and Henry had inhaled. Later, when Sabrina helped Lyla load the dishwasher in the kitchen, away from the men who were having brandy by the pool, she complimented Lyla on the dinner and for daring to experiment with guests, something Sabrina couldn't imagine doing.

"Oh, dear, I think I've made that seafood casserole about one hundred times in the past forty years. The secret is the Ritz crackers on top with loads of melted butter. Evan just doesn't remember. It's part of the Alzheimer's."

Sabrina worried when Detective Janquar took a step toward Lyla, but his voice was surprisingly gentle. "Ma'am, I am Detective Leon Janquar—"

Janquar was interrupted by Rory Eagan, who had stormed up the driveway from his house below, indignation written all over the scowl on his otherwise handsome, smooth-featured face.

"What the hell is going on?" Rory asked.

Sabrina knew Rory was more inclined to bellow than speak. His flair for the dramatic annoyed her. She was glad his house sat down on a slope below Villa Mascarpone. She could go weeks without seeing him, though she saw his wife frequently. Sabrina had become friends with Mara, meeting her first through Henry and later through Lyla's newly formed reading group.

Janquar looked at Rory and then over to Lyla.

"A crime was committed here, ma'am," the officer told Lyla, ignoring Rory. "I can't tell you much more right now, but an officer will be over to your house within the next several hours to interview you, and we may be able to provide more information then. I'd ask you to please go to your home and remain there for now."

"What, and not know what's going on in our own neighborhood? Officer, I have a wife and two children who live next door. I demand to know if they are at risk," Rory said, pointing a finger at Janquar. Sabrina caught a faint whiff of rum from Rory and noticed a redness to his tanned checks.

"Listen, Mr. Eagan, everything is under control here. No one is at risk, but this is an official crime scene, and I must insist you return to your home and let my men do their job." Janquar stepped in front of Rory.

Sabrina saw Evan come up behind Lyla, placing his hand on her right shoulder.

"Come on, dear, let's wait at home to find out what's happening," Evan said, pulling Lyla gently toward him.

"Thanks, folks," Janquar said.

"Well, do you think you could at least move your vehicle so I can get out of my driveway? I have an important appointment I can't miss," Rory told Janquar, grabbing his keys from his pocket.

"Sure thing, after you give a brief statement about whether you might have seen anything unusual, and as long as you understand we'll need to interview you in more detail first thing tomorrow," Janquar said, motioning to one of the officers to move the cruiser.

They watched Rory gesture as he talked to a different cop before trotting down the driveway to get his Suburban.

Janquar winked at Lyla and then looked over toward Neil.

"We don't want to be responsible for an empty stool down at Bar None, now do we?"

Thinking she should take advantage of the lightness of the moment, Sabrina asked Janquar if she could leave, reminding him that there were new guests arriving at the dock who had reservations for Villa Mascarpone she needed to divert.

"There's no reason to detain my client, is there, Detective?" Neil said, making it sound more like a statement than a question.

"Just as long as she doesn't go off-island. I'll want her to come to the station for questioning first thing in the morning, and I'll want the information about where the victim lives phoned in right away," Janquar told Neil Perry.

"What do I have to be questioned about? I've told you everything I know."

"You were the last person to see this guy alive, as far as I know, and the first to find him dead. That's reason enough, Ms. Salter."

Chapter Four

Henry arrived at Tide-Away to find Scott lying naked on a lounge chair, save for the tiny towel he had draped over his twinkie. He had slicked enough sun tan oil on him that if you threw him in a frying pan, he'd sauté.

The thoughts Henry harbored the night before about devouring Scott for twenty-four hours straight were no longer appetizing. He could distract himself with an occasional fling, but Henry craved routine, the predictability that came with the monotony of monogamy. Normal. Could he just have an ordinary life? Now with a murder at Villa Mascarpone, the tectonic plates of the new world he'd created had shifted. He was back in turbulent skies and needed to fasten his seatbelt.

"Hey, where'd you go?" Scott asked, lifting his Dolce & Gabbana sunglasses so he could look Henry directly in the eye.

"Sorry, but you're going to have to leave," Henry said, ignoring Scott's question. He had more important things to think about, like how he was going to get Tide-Away ready in record time. He figured the first thing he'd do was strip the bed they'd slept on and get the sheets in the washer. They hadn't made much of a mess of the house where they'd crashed after a romantic dinner on the patio at Asolare the evening before. But Henry needed to make sure the house was perfect for the couple who were not going to stay in the villa they had reserved and whom he didn't want disappointed with the substitute.

One of the fringe benefits from Ten Villas was use of any villa that was unoccupied, as long as he restored it to a guest-worthy state when he was done. The lure of a luxury villa with hot tub and pool was hard to say no to, Henry had learned. But it was not the white picket fence life he longed for.

Straight people didn't get it. They equated a gay life with South Beach and a flamboyant lifestyle. What Henry had hoped he would have with David was a couple of kids and a golden retriever to go with a weathered, gray-shingled cottage surrounded by a picket fence. But that had been before David betrayed him.

"Is something wrong?" Scott said, sitting up straight in the deck chair with exaggerated concern.

"Honey, this has nothing to do with you. I just have to get this house ready for guests, pronto. They were supposed to stay somewhere else, but it's still occupied," Henry said. The inevitable boredom that ultimately fizzled his infatuations had been accelerated by the death of Carter Johnson at Villa Mascarpone. Henry wondered what it would be like to have a steady significant other in his life when faced with a crisis. He just wasn't into this boy-toy scene.

"Okay, I'll just slip into the shower," Scott said.

"No time for that," Henry said, thinking about how long it would take to scrub all that suntan oil out of the tile shower stall.

"Well, I'll just take a quick dip then," Scott said, starting to walk toward the hexagonal shaped pool.

"Are you kidding? I'd have to call the company that cleaned up after BP in the Panhandle," Henry said, beginning to straighten the six teak deck chairs so they were in a perfect chorus line.

Scott stood and watched while Henry moved over to the round patio table where they had sipped champagne under the stars. Henry was all business, pushing in each chair and picking up the acrylic flutes reserved for outdoor use, which had toppled over. Scott's pout rivaled that of a two-year-old who'd had his binky stolen.

"I can't leave like this," he said, sweeping his hands from his arms down to his legs over his shiny body.

Henry strode over to the side of the house and turned on the outdoor shower. Getting rid of Scott was more work than cleaning the house.

"Here, rinse off and hurry," he said. "I'll bring a towel out after I load the dishwasher."

Henry placed the flutes and a few other dishes in the dishwasher and wondered how Sabrina was faring. He hated the way the cops were all over her. He remembered how they had treated her when they had a burglary at one of the villas, letting her know they didn't approve of her and what had happened in Nantucket. He couldn't imagine being the subject of their scrutiny.

He grabbed a clean fluffy towel and rushed out to the patio to find Scott. Henry wrapped the towel around Scott, gently dabbing him dry.

"There you go, handsome. That's better, isn't it?" Henry asked.

"That's more like it," Scott said, stepping into the clothes Henry handed him.

"Look, sweetie, I'm really sorry I've got to give you the bum's rush here, but I've got kind of a work emergency," Henry said. "I'll call you later and make it up to you." He patted Scott on the tush and dashed back into the house, knowing he would never lay eyes on him again.

Chapter Five

Sabrina raced down the dirt road, which clung to the edge of the cliff where Villa Mascarpone and the other two villas were perched. Tourists were horrified when they first encountered the loose gravel surface without a guardrail to protect them from falling three hundred feet down onto jagged rocks and coral. Sabrina could drive it with her eyes closed with no fear. It wasn't natural danger that scared her. No, what kept her awake at night was all man-made.

She made it up the next hillside where her own small house sat tucked in a pocket surrounded by thick vegetation on three sides, facing the Caribbean on the fourth. Normally, it took her eight minutes to drive back from Villa Mascarpone. This afternoon she made it in five. Neil's final words, whispered as he walked her away from the cops and over to her jeep, propelled her to rush home. Besides, there were no cops to give her a speeding ticket. They were all back at Villa Mascarpone.

"And Salty, one last little bit of advice. If you have anything in your house you don't want the cops to see, maybe some homegrown weed, maybe something more exciting, get rid of it. I'd bet you a month of free mojitos they'll have a search warrant by tomorrow morning," he'd said.

Weed wasn't her thing, and for the most part, except when people around her were getting killed, her life was beautifully boring. But there were a few things Sabrina didn't want the cops to see, and the first was the Villa Mascarpone file.

She pulled into her driveway behind an ancient red Wrangler, which belonged to Tanya from Texas. Tanya was one of the many minions who passed through Ten Villas in an effort to live in St. John. Like most, Tanya had arrived for a vacation, fallen in love with the island, and on a drunken last evening, called home and instructed whomever she was leaving behind to sell everything and send her a check. She wasn't coming back. Until island living got too tough, which it almost always did. Jubilation turned to depression when island refugees realized you had to go to St. Thomas to get to a Kmart and San Juan to gamble. Boredom and isolation drove them home, making room for a new crop of dropouts. So far, Tanya had stuck it out.

Sabrina's heart leapt at the sight of a shiny-coated chocolate lab bolting through the pet flap in her front door. This was the only creature she had ever been able to live with in total harmony.

"Hey, Girlfriend," Sabrina said, dropping to her knees, letting the dog nuzzle her neck. If only people could be like dogs, she thought, not for the first time. Girlfriend was Sabrina's first dog. She had vowed never to be tied down to one, until one day when Henry surprised her with a small ball of fur.

"You said you never have girlfriends," Henry had told her. He'd been horrified when she claimed not to have had a single female friend in the past two decades, only male pals—and most of them had hung her out to dry.

"Her name's Girlfriend, so now you've got one," Henry had said, turning to leave before Sabrina had a chance to protest.

Since then, Sabrina had started to warm to the idea of having girlfriends. She liked Mara Bennett, whom she sensed was an independent woman living under difficult circumstances. Lyla Banks was becoming her friend. The tall, graceful, and brave woman was inspirational, a role model for aging for a motherless woman like Sabrina.

Girlfriend followed her into the house where Tanya stood before a commercial-size stove, removing an assortment of appetizers from the oven to deliver to guests. She looked ready to pack up and leave, Sabrina noted with relief.

"Hey, Tanya, everything okay here?" Sabrina asked, not expecting anything else could go wrong.

"Everything is okay, except a woman called. What a witch with a *b*, if you'll excuse me for saying," Tanya said.

"Who was she?"

"She said she owns Villa Mascarpone and wants to talk to you, pronto." Tanya piled the hors d'oeuvres she had removed from the oven into Pyrex containers, ready for her to deliver to the guests at Lime Cay villa.

"Oh sh—," Sabrina said, almost forgetting to respect that born-again Tanya didn't allow cussing.

Sabrina knew she'd have to disregard her lawyer's advice and the police's order to not discuss the case with anyone. She needed to talk to Angela Martino about the murder that had occurred in the villa she owned. Maybe Angela had already heard. Was word out? Sabrina reigned herself in, concentrating on the first step she had to take to protect herself.

As soon as Tanya had left with the trays and containers placed in her vehicle, Sabrina walked over to the side of the main room of her tiny three-room cottage. Houses on St. John ranged from $800,000 to $8,000,000. Sabrina had nothing left after she had fed the bloodthirsty lawyers in Nantucket. Even after she sold the Beacon Hill townhouse and the infamous scene of the crime in Nantucket, she was broke. She declined the book offers and the paid television appearances because she'd rather be accused of murdering her husband than pander as a media whore. When she learned her husband had named her as a beneficiary on one of his life insurance policies, which she hadn't known existed and was the only policy not bound by the terms of his divorce to be for the benefit of his kids, Sabrina took it as a heavenly sign that she should take the money and run.

While Henry had chosen to purchase a condo more luxurious than the cottage she had purchased for about the same money, Sabrina was thrilled with the tiny house where she had no neighbors and where no one could tell her what color to paint her front door.

She opened a file cabinet drawer where she kept her business records and reached for the folder labeled "Villa Mascarpone." She found the printed-out e-mails she had received from Carter Johnson when he'd rented the villa, copies of the lease agreement, and a bank check he had used to pay for the house. Unlike most people, Carter Johnson had paid in full in advance rather than just sending the required deposit. He'd done this because he'd only booked the rental four weeks in advance when Sabrina had an unexpected cancellation.

She looked for a mailing address on the e-mails but there was none. The only phone number was for a mobile phone. The bank check was from American Express. There was nothing here that would help her or the police notify Johnson's relatives about his murder.

Sabrina grabbed the sparse information she had about Carter Johnson, taking note of the receipt for the propane refill for the gas grill with a post-it stuck to it with a note in her handwriting. She was owed twenty-seven dollars for the refill she had purchased at St. John Hardware during Carter's visit, when he'd forgotten to turn the tank off and had run out mid-vacation. She knew that tank of propane could cost her a lot more than twenty-seven bucks if the cops learned she had been to Villa Mascarpone while Carter Johnson stayed there, especially after she'd lied to them and told them she'd met him only once.

No one knew except Carter, and he was dead, so it had really been smarter to not mention it. It wasn't a big deal. All she had done was deliver the filled tank to him. They'd barely talked. She ripped the receipt into tiny pieces and then set fire to them in her sink. Then she ran the faucet full blast, washing away any remains of what could tie her to Carter Johnson.

Chapter Six

Sabrina cruised down the hill and then up and over several others in the large van they used to pick up guests at the ferry in downtown Cruz Bay, the center of St. John. By the time she arrived, Cruz Bay was bustling as much as any Caribbean island ever bustles. Sabrina had heard about the time some politician thought Cruz Bay needed a traffic light. Apparently, the island came as close to a revolution as it had since the days of the great slave rebellion against the Danish three hundred years before.

Sabrina circled around the crowded streets that led to the dock where the ferry from St. Thomas arrived and dumped tourists onto St. John several times each day. Although Sabrina appreciated tourism, as it was now her livelihood, she privately thanked the ferry for removing the same amount of visitors off the island on the return trip. Sabrina knew that tourists were essential to the economic survival of St. John, but they were slowly destroying the island. Even here, life had its Draconian choices.

She found a space and backed in the van, nestling it between two flatbed trucks, converted into Safari trucks by adding benches to give tourists "the best tour" of St. John. Ten Villa's official meet-and-greet vehicle was a van large enough for the multiple suitcases tourists insisted on bringing, even though on St. John, you could easily survive a week's vacation with a pair of shorts, a T-shirt, a swimsuit, and flip-flops.

Sabrina thought of the luggage sitting in Carter Johnson's jeep, the clothes packed, never to be worn again, and for the first time, she felt sadness sweep over her, followed by a rush of rage. St. John had promised her a new future, not more trouble. Sure, there was some small-time drug dealing. What island didn't have it? And there had been the occasional break-in. But a murder? On St. John? She felt betrayed. She had fled to and chosen this island as her home, her sanctuary.

Sabrina was on the verge of tears, a rare good cry, which was not going to be helpful when she had to meet and greet the new arrivals.

She knew strolling over to Bar None for a quick drink wasn't an option. She watched herself that way. Drinking was a way of life on an island, probably because almost everyone here had come to escape from somewhere, someone, or something. Sometimes from all three. It was okay to drink enough to be numb but not enough to duplicate the same kind of problems you were trying to leave behind.

She decided to play a game she and Henry liked to amuse themselves with while they waited for guests to arrive at the dock. They would try to match the names of their clients to the tourists milling about the dock. Today she was meeting Deirdre and Sam Leonard, who were arriving to spend two weeks at Villa Mascarpone, or so they thought. They were coming from Massachusetts, where Sabrina had grown up, gone to college, and never thought she would leave. This should be easy, she thought. Preppy never went out of style in New England. She watched for green whales on navy blue cotton, Madras Bermuda shorts, anything nautical.

Sabrina, holding a Ten Villas sign, was surprised to see the Leonards approach her from the direction of Bar None, not from the dock. She pegged the around forty-five strawberry blonde in a pair of white capris and a blue-and-white-striped jersey as Deirdre, more by the color of her hair than by her outfit. Packed with Irish descendants, Boston was the redhead capitol of the United States, and strawberry blonde was just a redhead's way of trying to go blonde. Sabrina wondered how much time someone with skin as fair as Deirdre's could spend on the beach, though she looked like she needed some color in her cheeks and fresh air.

"We caught an earlier ferry and decided to have our first margarita while we waited for you," she said, smiling at Sabrina.

Sam Leonard, a tall string bean of a guy with not a stitch of preppy clothing on him, shook her hand and helped load the six bags he and Deirdre were dragging into the van. Deirdre climbed into the backseat, while Sam and Sabrina hopped into the front, escaping the madness of Cruz Bay as she drove them up one block to St. John Car Rental, where a Jeep Cherokee awaited them. Now was the time for Sabrina to break the news to the vacationing couple, who seemed more subdued than most people on arrival.

"Did you have a good trip?" Sabrina asked, wanting to know if any ire from travel complications would bubble up when she told the Leonards they would be spending their vacation in a different house than they had booked.

"It was just long, really long," Deirdre said, yawning.

"I'm not sure what the airlines can take away next," Sam said. "I'm starving and stiff, but at least we're here." He looked behind him at his wife.

"You holding up okay?" Sam asked Deirdre.

Sabrina stiffened. Apparently the Leonards were one of those rare couples. The ones that last. Sabrina could always peg them, but she would never be part of one, she knew. It just wasn't in her horoscope or her biology.

"I just want to get to the house," Deirdre said.

Sabrina saw her opportunity.

"Well, I have some great news for you about the house. You've been upgraded to the magnificent Villa Tide-Away at no extra cost. We're delighted to offer this opportunity to you as first-time guests of Ten Villas, and we're adding some complimentary extra services. We'll be providing a full course gourmet dinner on the night of your choice and maid service all week long," she said, beaming with benevolence.

"No, thank you, Sabrina. I want to go to Villa Mascarpone, as planned," Deirdre said firmly from the backseat.

"We appreciate your kind offer but we chose Villa Mascarpone for some very special reasons," Sam said, sending a nervous glance back to his wife.

The day had gone from bad to worse, Sabrina decided.

"Oh, but you'll have a hot tub and Jacuzzi, a wet bar at the pool, and so much more at Tide-Away. The décor in the house is by far the best on the island, with native-crafted mahogany furniture done by local artists. We're only able to offer you the house because of a last-minute cancellation. You will just adore the sunsets from the balcony off the master bedroom suite," Sabrina said, realizing now she sounded like a voiceover on the Travel Channel.

"No. I want to go to Villa Mascarpone," Deirdre said like a petulant child.

"She's the boss," Sam said, shrugging his shoulders while he gave one of those glances at Sabrina that said, "And I know better than to argue with the boss."

Sabrina pulled into the parking lot of the car rental agency, which was so tiny you often had to wait for them to move one of the thirty-odd cars so you could fit in. She placed the van in park, leaving the air conditioner running because she had a feeling it was about to get a lot hotter than tropical after hearing Deirdre's insistence.

"Folks, I am sorry, but you can't stay at Villa Mascarpone. It's not possible," she said, knowing they would demand to know why and not knowing if she had a fresh lie to hand them. Henry was so much better at this. All those years working as a flight attendant in first class had trained him how to deal with people who are simply pains in the ass.

"We have a contract, Sabrina. We paid a deposit. We are going to stay at Villa Mascarpone," Deirdre said in a voice that meant business.

"I wish you could, but the guest before you has been incapacitated and is unable to leave," Sabrina said, giving it a last go. She was tired, exhausted by the day's events, and had nothing left to give the Leonards. She was due at Bar None so she could talk with Neil. These people were only here for a vacation. Couldn't they give it up?

"What do you mean the last guest is still there?" Sam asked, sounding like he could be as demanding as his wife.

"But that can't be. We booked the next two weeks there," Deirdre said. Sabrina wanted to know why this middle-aged couple from Boston who had never been on St. John before couldn't just be grateful for an upgrade to an opulent villa and be done with it.

"Well, I'm afraid that's how it is. Look, you're going to hear this anyway. The man in Villa Mascarpone died. The police are investigating. They won't allow you there. I'm sorry, but I think you'll be even happier at Tide-Away," she said.

"He died?" Deirdre asked.

"You can't mean that," Sam said, turning to look back at Deirdre.

"How did he die? Did he have some kind of accident?" Deirdre asked.

"All I can tell you is that the police are treating it as a crime scene. I'm sorry. I realize this is an unpleasant way to start your vacation. But you really will love Tide-Away and the extra services we're providing you," Sabrina said. If they were this upset hearing about the death of the previous guest in the house they booked, surely they would want to stay somewhere else.

"A crime scene? What kind of a crime scene?" Deirdre wasn't going to let go, Sabrina could see.

"Honey, this isn't Sabrina's fault. Let's go to Tide-Away for now and sort it out," Sam said, reaching over to the backseat for Deirdre's hand.

Chapter Seven

Sabrina felt the eyes of the entire crowd at Bar None as she walked past the bar, filled to capacity with happy hour customers, and straight over to what everyone called "the Office," Neil Perry's corner of the bar. Bar None was right on the beach in Cruz Bay. Here, people fell off the ferry and within a few steps could sit drinking a margarita, mojito, or beer while soaking in paradise with their feet in the sand. The roof of the bar, made of stretched sail canvases, gave just enough protection from the sun or an errant tropical shower. You could sit at the long oval bar or at one of the battered booths. The far corner one was dedicated as Neil Perry's office. He'd traded one bar for another two years ago, dropping out of the practice of criminal law in LA. There were rumors as to why he'd left, but Sabrina was the last one to ask questions.

He was on the phone when she slid onto the bench opposite his. He held his right index finger to his mouth, signaling her to be silent. Sabrina folded her arms across her chest. She needed a drink and started to slip out of the bench when Neil hung up.

"Hey, where you going? We've got work to do, Salty."

"I'm just getting a drink. Hold on, will you? And don't call me that."

"No drinking 'til after the meeting. Then you can drink yourself silly and we'll call Henry to drive you home, but we got to set priorities here," Neil said, drawing the straw pull shades down around the booth.

"We need some privacy for this meeting," he said.

"Privacy? Sure, we have a fat chance of that on this island."

"Listen, I'm just trying to help you here, Sabrina. Henry called me. I didn't go looking to get involved here in what is pretty clearly a homicide. But hey, if you don't need or want my help, if you'd rather contact that fancy barracuda who represented you in the Nantucket case . . . what was her name? Why can't I think of it? It was on national television every night for about a year and a half," Neil said, leaning forward with his fingers folded together.

"Justine Mercy, and no, I do not want to call her," Sabrina said, sitting back down and settling onto the bench where she knew she had to endure recounting her story.

"Is that her real name or is it made-up?" Neil asked, relaxing back onto his bench. He leaned over and lifted the straw shade. "Hey, someone, get us a fresh pot of coffee over here, will you?"

Sabrina ignored his question about her last attorney's identity. She never wanted to see that woman again or any of the other members of her so-called dream team. She just wanted to be left alone, renting and cleaning her ten little villas, not doing anything to warrant any attention. She wanted to be invisible.

"Okay, now, as I remember, the last time I acted briefly as your lawyer, which I did pro bono, by the way, one of your villas had been burglarized, correct?" Neil pulled out a stack of paper place mats and began to make notes in pencil on the back of one.

"You never sent me a bill. You only represented me for a couple of hours, when I had a second meeting with the cops, remember?" Sabrina had paid some astronomical legal fees over the years and was incensed Neil Perry was suggesting she had dodged his.

"No, no, Salty, don't go getting dramatic. I considered it a courtesy to a new resident on the island. Plus, I thought you were good looking. Besides, you bought me dinner that night, and didn't we go swimming afterward?"

Sabrina rolled her eyes. She remembered the swim well and how she'd almost let her guard down with Neil. He was an attractive man, but was any man worth what she'd been through in Nantucket? "Please, can we get on with this?"

"Sure. I just know from that little incident about the burglary that the island cops aren't particularly thrilled you chose St. John as your new home. Probably in part because Attorney Mercy made the Nantucket cops look dumber than Whitey Bulger made the FBI look in front of the entire world. So I want to be very careful here. I need your story. Actually, stories. I need to know all about the then and the now."

Neil accepted a tray with a decanter and two white porcelain mugs on it with a pitcher of milk and a bowl of sugar packets. He poured a mug and slid it over to Sabrina. She wanted to decline the coffee, show that she was tough and that she didn't need any accommodations, but the smell was too divine to resist.

"Cream? Sugar?" Neil asked.

Sabrina shook her head and took a gulp. The strong hot black coffee warmed her body.

"Okay, let's start with the now. Tell me everything you did today, starting with waking up. Don't spare me a single boring or titillating detail," Neil said, taking a sip from his own mug.

"I got up at five forty-five like I always do," Sabrina said, hating having to share the details of her private life with anyone, even someone who couldn't reveal them under the attorney–client privilege.

"Five forty-five? A.M.? For real, Salty?" Neil asked, as if this was just the first thing she had to say that he would doubt.

"Yeah, for real. Now, do you want me to go on?"

"Yeah, yeah. It's just so early," Neil said.

"I watched the sunrise, did a little yoga and meditation, then took Girlfriend out for a walk," Sabrina said, pouring another cup of coffee out of the carafe into her mug.

"Girlfriend? You have a girlfriend? Listen, you aren't . . . haven't switched teams because of that mess in Massachusetts, have you?" Neil asked, his voice crackling with the huskiness Sabrina had found sexy the last time he'd been her lawyer of the hour.

"My dog, Neil. My dog's name is Girlfriend, remember?"

"The one we went swimming with after you bought me dinner that night? We were pretty drunk, so you can't blame me for forgetting her name. At least I remembered yours, right? Go on, I won't interrupt you anymore." Neil picked up his pencil and began to jot down notes as Sabrina described making coffee and taking appetizers out of the freezer and putting them into the refrigerator so that Tanya could bake and deliver them later in the day to guests staying at Lime Cay. She continued to torture him with the details about which cleaning items she loaded in her bucket and which book she downloaded onto her iPod.

"Okay, Salty, get to the part about when you found the body," Neil said, looking her dead in the eyes. Sabrina wondered if he was trying to intimidate her.

She told him exactly what she had told the police and added that she had called Henry to join her at Villa Mascarpone because she was leery of being with the cops alone after last time. She guessed Henry had the same concern, which is why he'd called Neil.

"What do you know about this guy, the murder victim?" Neil asked.

Sabrina took a breath before answering, reaching into the navy-blue-and-white-striped canvas bag she called her briefcase.

"Not much. It's all here," she said, pulling out the Villa Mascarpone file. "His name is Carter Johnson. He was a last-minute booking, so he got a discount but had to pay the entire rental upfront. He sent an American Express check. We communicated only by e-mail. Since I got the check via overnight delivery, I wasn't worried. Besides, I had his cell phone number. I was just relieved to be booking the house. Someone had canceled for the two weeks he took them and the following two. I wasn't looking forward to explaining a four-week vacancy to the owner. She's not exactly sweetness and light. I was lucky to fill all four weeks."

Neil took the file and glanced at the printed e-mails, the executed rental agreement, and the copy of the check. He flipped each piece of paper so he could examine the backside.

"This is it?" he asked.

"Yes. What more should there be? He was just renting a vacation house, not applying for a passport," Sabrina said, crossing her legs so that Neil couldn't see the left one was shaking.

"And you met him only once? When you picked him up at the ferry?"

Did he know somehow that she had brought the propane tank to the house? No, how could he? She kept with her little lie. Consistency was the key to lying, she fig-ured. Telling the truth about going to the house would only complicate matters. It would give the cops a reason to think that somehow she was involved with this guy. And it wasn't true, so what was the harm in a small fib? She could always say she'd forgotten, if need be. She filled people's propane tanks all the time.

"Yes, just the once," she said, squeezing her right calf against her left leg, begging it silently to stay still.

"Okay, now tell me about Nantucket," Neil said, pushing his coffee mug to the side and pulling out a fresh placemat to write on.

"Not until you switch the coffee for vodka," Sabrina said, sliding her mug over next to his.

Chapter Eight

Henry looked around Bar None to see if Sabrina was there. He'd spotted her jeep in the parish priest's parking spot outside the church across the street, even though there was a sign posted, "Thou shalt not park here." Sometimes he worried that Sabrina was a little self-destructive. Then again, she seemed to think she was predestined for disaster.

Henry wasn't much of a drinker, but tonight was an exception. The sight of Carter Johnson flopped on the sagging hammock, bloody and lifeless, made him sick and weary. Life was not supposed to be so complicated here.

Henry sidled up to the bar, which was nearly full, and ordered a mojito and a plate of coconut shrimp as an afterthought. He hadn't eaten since dinner at Asolare.

He looked around him and knew why Sabrina liked Bar None. The music was too loud to have any kind of a real conversation. She could sip her drink here, look out at Cruz Bay, and be left alone. How someone who had gone to such extremes to be left alone managed to keep walking into other people's disasters, he didn't know.

The bartender slid a drink in front of him, telling him his shrimp order would be right up. He heard the loud voice of a man he could not see about eight stools down from him. It could only be one guy.

"Someone turn down that blasted music and turn on the six o'clock news so we can find out what the hell is going on here, will you?"

Henry leaned forward and looked down the bar, past the platter of shrimp the bartender had just slid in front of him, at Rory Eagan, who nodded at him. Henry noticed that Rory, dressed in Madras Bermuda shorts and a blue button-down collar shirt with the sleeves rolled up far enough to show tanned arms donning a Rolex, looked more like a gay man than most gay men did.

"Hey, Villa Mascarpone is one of your villas, isn't it?" Rory asked. "What happened there? The cops won't tell me even though I practically live next door."

Rory Eagan typified the kind of jerk Henry no longer had to cater to as he had when he'd worked as a flight attendant for twelve years in first class.

Now he only had to meet them at the dock and take them to their villas. Short and sweet.

"No clue," Henry said, stuffing a hot coconut shrimp into his mouth so he wouldn't have to talk to Rory. He looked up at the oversized flat screen and feigned interest in the weather forecast. It was always eighty-six degrees with a 30 percent chance of an occasional shower in St. John this time of year. Channel 8 was interviewing some politician about an upcoming festival in St. Thomas. Nothing about a murder.

Henry was relieved to see Rory Eagan was now preoccupied with two young female tourists not much older than his twins. He felt sorry for the kids, having such a jerk for a father. He thought about his own father, an airline pilot 'til he retired. Hank Whitman wasn't an easy man to be the son of, particularly the gay son, but he had been a decent man and would never have been found pawing young women in a bar, knowing his kids could easily wander by and see him in all his glory.

Why Mara Bennett, the island's most successful (and only female) builder, had married such a miscreant had escaped Henry until he became close friends with her.

They'd had coffee a dozen or more times before Mara admitted to Henry just how aware she was of Rory's "whoring," as she called it. It turned out she didn't care. Rory had turned up on St. John as a down-on-his-luck widower with a young set of boy-girl twins. Their drunken mother had driven straight into a tree, handing Rory a sad story that Mara knew played well with the single women on St. John. She never believed that Rory loved her. She knew he'd married her for her money, and she'd married him for his beautiful young children, with whom she had immediately fallen in love. Mara told Henry she got the better end of the deal.

The bartender reached up to grab a bottle of Stoli Citros, a couple of glasses, and a bowl filled with sliced lemons and carried them over to Neil's office. The bamboo shades were pulled down so Henry couldn't see who was inside, but he guessed it must be Sabrina. She needed more than a bottle of Stoli to get through this one. Neil must have been interviewing her for hours.

The other bartender had turned up the volume of the television, which hushed most of the people at the bar. A woman with a snarl on her face and a stiff blonde hairstyle that resembled a helmet began to speak in a blistering tirade.

"Breaking news tonight. Reports that Sabrina Salter has yet another body at her feet. Unconfirmed reports tonight are that on a remote Caribbean Island where she fled, another murder victim has been discovered. Not just discovered, ladies and gentlemen, but discovered by *her*. We also understand that even though Sabrina Salter has not been charged as of this moment, that even though she has not been named as a party of interest, she has lawyered up, folks. We're working on talking to her lawyer and getting more information for you. How history does repeat itself. I wonder how that Nantucket jury will feel hearing this news."

The bar crowd went silent as former prosecutor now investigative journalist Faith Chase showed video clips of a different Sabrina, a more professionally dressed woman, first on air, reporting snowfall amounts in various Massachusetts communities after a blizzard. "Worcester takes the prize with over twenty-eight inches," Sabrina told the camera. Next, a Sabrina coming out of a courthouse, head ducked down, flanked by several lawyers after her arraignment for first-degree murder, followed by some tender shots of Sabrina's dead husband's children at his funeral. Finally, a clip of Sabrina emerging once again from the same courthouse after her acquittal, repeating the mantra, "No comment, no comment, no comment."

"Will she get away with it again, folks? Will Sabrina Salter just wander from island to island, killing off the men in her life? Stay tuned. We are on this story and will provide you, our wonderful fans, with the same determined, dogged reporting you have come to trust."

Henry watched the jaw-jutting, hissing Faith Chase sign off with, "Good night and God bless each and every one of you for caring about the victims of crime."

The bartender flipped off the television and answered a phone before turning the familiar sound of Bob Marley back on. Henry felt sick, the coconut shrimp and mojito definitely not liking what they'd just heard. Sabrina had shared with him the horrors of being demonized by the goddess of trash TV, confiding that her most frightening dreams were not about the shooting or the trial but about Faith Chase vilifying her every act each night before a national audience. If she wore a plain navy-blue skirt with a white blouse and a pair of pearls to court, she was trying to look like a parochial school sophomore. If she wore a black suit, she was shooting for the "don't blame me, I'm the widow" appeal.

Henry had come to St. John because of Sabrina. She had convinced him the island was a perfect place to start over, leave behind the heartbreak and sorrow, the disappointment and damage. But her demons wouldn't be banished; they just kept following her wherever she went. Henry couldn't help but wonder if his demons would be any kinder. He doubted it and ordered another drink. This time, his father's favorite, a double Scotch on the rocks, while he tried not to think about what David, his ex, was doing at this moment.

He looked over at Rory Eagan, a horrible excuse for a father, husband, and man, and realized David had been no better. His promises to leave his wife, acknowledge his love for Henry, and start a family were all lies. And even on the perfect island in paradise, there was no escape from betrayal.

Then Henry wondered for the first time where Rory Eagan had been that morning.

Chapter Nine

Neil poked his head around the bamboo shade that separated his office from the other booths at Bar None.

"Hey, Mitch," he hollered, "bring me a bottle of Stoli Citros, a couple of glasses, and some ice." He had such a sexy voice, a little on the hoarse side, Sabrina noticed again—not that she wanted to.

"And lemons," Sabrina said. She loved lemons. Lemons with butter, lemon frosting, lemon poppy seed muffins, and most of all, lemons with her booze.

"Oh, yeah, and some lemons, a lot of lemons," Neil said, sitting back on the bench. "Okay, Salty, you'll have your Stoli and your lemons. I think I even see Henry sitting out there at the bar, ready to drive you home when we're done. So, the Nantucket story. Shoot."

Neil winced before the double entendre even occurred to Sabrina and apologized, grabbing the bottle, ice bucket, and glasses from the bartender.

"I'll be right back with the lemons," Mitch said, looking at her with that funny expression she remembered seeing on faces ever since Nantucket. People never looked at you the same once they knew you'd been connected with a murder. You were forever distinguished from the rest of the population, who got their murder thrills on television and from novels. You became a story, a legend of sorts, and you could never shake it.

Neil poured a tumbler full of vodka and slipped three ice cubes on the top.

"Here, Salty, you look like you could use this," he said, sliding the drink over to her. Then he poured an identical drink for himself.

"I could have used it a couple of hours ago," Sabrina said, taking the bowl of lemon wedges directly from Mitch, squeezing three over her drink, and gulping about a third of it in one sip.

Neil watched her with those smoky blue eyes of his, blue like the Atlantic Ocean in New England. Sabrina didn't want to look into his blues while she told him her very old, very sad story. She hated talking about Nantucket, almost as much as she detested talking about Allerton, the lonely long peninsula south of Boston where she'd grown up.

"We owned a house on Nantucket. We used it mostly in the summer together, always inviting lots of people over. But I liked it better in the off season, after the throngs of beautiful people were gone." She added more ice to her drink so she didn't pass out before she was done talking.

She hadn't eaten recently, since she'd skipped breakfast before heading up to clean Villa Mascarpone.

Sabrina took a deep breath and decided to just spit it out. Better to rip a bandage off quickly. Then the pain would be fast and short.

"Okay, here's what happened. I met my husband while I was working at Channel Three as a meteorologist. Ben was the sports anchor for Channel Three. He was funny, handsome, a local celebrity. *Boston Magazine* always named him as the best sports anchor in Boston. We were at work one evening when Ben was served with divorce papers. He was married to Cyndi Cashman, a consumer reporter over at Channel Eight. They were in the news all of the time and when they had kids, the media were all over them. He thought they were the perfect family. Until that night," Sabrina said, finishing her drink and handing Neil the empty glass.

Neil put up his right index finger, signaling her to hit the pause button for a moment.

"Hey, Mitch, bring another bucket of ice. And a couple of orders of onion rings and conch fritters, will you?" Neil turned back to her. Had he heard her stomach growling? Or did Neil Perry have a sense about her, one Sabrina remembered vaguely from the night on the beach when they'd flopped on the still warm sand and had almost gotten a little too familiar?

"This was his second marriage. He'd left wife number one for Cyndi, and when Cyndi left him, Ben was devastated. I don't think he'd ever been rejected before. He turned to me for consolation and I was flattered. He told me I had more depth, was more of a woman than anyone he'd ever met before. When he came on to me, I wasn't smart enough to say no. I mean, at the time, I bought the story. I had been so much more supportive and caring than Cyndi ever had been. He told me he loved me as he had never loved before," Sabrina said, embarrassed at how cliché her story was.

"And you believed you understood him the way no other woman had ever been able to in the past," Neil said, handing her another drink.

"Of course. I was an idiot. In my defense, I was about fifteen years younger than Ben, but still, I should have seen it. He was on the rebound. I was ten years younger than Cyndi and he knew that would bother her." She couldn't admit to Neil that she had met Cyndi on a number of occasions and thought she seemed okay, not the demonic woman Ben had described her to be. But Ben had been so convincing, and she'd wanted to believe him so much that she figured Cyndi was just a phony. After all, Ben had captured her heart. He was the only person who had ever told her that he loved her. The only person. Ever.

She had never told anyone this. Not Justine Mercy, who had saved her from a murder conviction. Not Henry, the only person on the planet she now trusted. And she was not going to share this with Neil Perry.

"So he married you on the rebound?" Neil asked.

"Yes. My ratings were pretty high at the time and I was getting good press. He liked being with someone who drew him additional publicity. I worshipped him and doted on his kids," Sabrina said, eyeing the huge platter Mitch was handing them under the office shade, the salty smell of grease wafting through the Caribbean breeze.

"I thought we were doing okay. We'd take his kids to the Red Sox, Patriots, and Bruins games and we were always being photographed by the press," Sabrina said, taking an onion ring and salting it before she popped it in her mouth. She hadn't minded the photographs, but she'd wondered, sometimes, how Ben's kids felt about being thrust into photos with their stepmother. She knew nothing about raising children, but she knew they were smarter than people gave them credit for. She had grown up motherless and knew it had been smart not to have children of her own. She was not mother material.

"And then?" Neil asked as he dipped a conch fritter into green habanera hot sauce.

"And then he did it again. Only this time, it was with an attorney who specialized in sports law."

"Sports law? What kind of woman specializes in jock wars?" Neil asked.

"An even younger than me, very confident, super-buff lawyer, that's who. I got an anonymous e-mail from someone telling me that Ben was at the Oak Bar at the Copley Plaza with her holding hands one night when I was working late at the station. I decided it was from a crank, but hey, I had to drive to our Beacon Hill townhouse, so why not stop by the Copley, even though it's not exactly on the way, and treat myself to a nightcap? I'd worked hard all night."

Sabrina remembered the night more vividly than yesterday, probably because she visited it every night in her sleep. She had been so sure it was a mistake. She'd sauntered into the Copley as if she had the key to the penthouse in her purse, planning to feign surprise at finding Ben and whatever sports contact he was having a business drink with and joining them. There were so many women in sports broadcasting these days. She was certain her tipster had simply misunderstood the nature of the meeting.

But it was Sabrina who had misunderstood. Poised and confident, she'd entered the bar, pausing behind a massive ornate oak pillar to catch her breath, when she saw him. He'd caught the hand of the woman he was seated across from in the midst of what appeared to be a very feminine gesture. He took her fingertips and placed them on his lips, just as he did with Sabrina when he would stop her mid-sentence and capture her expressive hand and softly kiss her fingertips. Sabrina would forget what she was talking about and could only think about how Ben's mouth might feel on other parts of her body. Neil didn't need to know about this part. He seemed pretty attentive to Sabrina's story, but lawyers, even retired beach bum lawyers, didn't really care about the sad stuff. They just wanted enough facts to get you off.

"I could tell it was a romantic rendezvous. I knew in one split second he was done with me, had moved on, and that our marriage was over. I felt like someone had split my sternum down the middle with a meat cleaver," Sabrina said, reaching for a lemon wedge and giving it a vicious squeeze over the conch fritter. Hot sauce, no matter what color, was highly overrated.

"So you ran away to Nantucket? Why not just boot the bastard when he tried to come home and pretend he was late at a meeting? Why did you have to run away?"

Sabrina could hear the television blaring from the bar and ice cubes tinkling over the laugher and chatter and wanted to end the conversation. She didn't want to have to be talking to a lawyer again. She'd only found the body.

"Because I was devastated, that's why. I really didn't believe he would do to me what he'd done to his first wife, especially after Cyndi had done it to him. I truly thought we had something different, that I was so special to him that he wouldn't consider straying." *I thought that he really loved me,* she didn't say.

Sabrina grabbed a napkin and dabbed at her mouth, not wanting to meet Neil's eyes and see what Sabrina expected might be pity or disdain at the sight of a smart woman who had been just as dumb as the legions before her. Just another dumped broad. A first-class chump.

"And so, what happened on Nantucket?" Neil asked, making her wonder if he was uncomfortable with the tiny speck of emotion she had shown.

"I grabbed a late flight out of Boston to Nantucket, took a cab to the house. It was freezing inside, so I put up the heat. I made myself a double martini, threw on Ben's sweatshirt and sweatpants, and drank alone in the kitchen. We'd done a spread in the *Globe* the summer before about cooking in our Nantucket cottage kitchen for a local charity. The kids helped us serve, and I was beginning to enjoy being a stepmom," Sabrina said.

"Did you shoot him coming into the kitchen from outside?" Neil asked, looking at the bottom of his empty glass before splashing a touch of vodka into it. He raised the bottle to her. She nodded and let him get her just a little more drunk, just enough so she could finish telling the story but not enough to get her maudlin and blathering.

"No, no, I made a second drink and found some extra blankets, went upstairs, and crawled into bed. I just couldn't get warm, and I couldn't seem to get drunk, try as I did. I was semicomatose finally when I heard someone coming up the old rickety staircase to the second floor. The house belonged to one of the original whaling captains. Everything in the house creaks. I thought I heard voices, but I couldn't really tell if it was the wind howling outside the window. I sat up and reached into the drawer of the nightstand where Ben always kept a gun. 'Just in case,' he always would say. I was terrified. I heard the sound of the bedroom doorknob being turned, and I raised and pointed the gun toward it. When it opened, I just pulled the trigger. It never occurred to me that Ben would bring a woman to our vacation home, although I learned differently later at the trial," Sabrina said, suddenly so tired she could have put her head on the table and slept the remainder of the night.

"When did you figure out it was your husband?" Neil asked. He had started to jot down notes on the place mats, making her wonder what he found relevant to the dead man in the hammock.

When had she figured out it was her husband? Sabrina would take the answer with her to her grave. On her better days, she was certain it had only been after she had turned on the light and realized the intruder was her husband and his jock lawyer. But in the thinnest hours of the night when she tossed and turned, Sabrina wondered if she had seen Ben's face and then fired or pulled the trigger in a moment of rage. She would never know. All she knew was that a jury had decided to believe her and not the jock lawyer, who had testified for the prosecution.

"When I heard shrieking from a woman and turned on the lamp to find Ben bleeding from the gut, still holding the hand of the screaming blonde as he slipped to the floor." Sabrina still marveled at how the sight of Ben entering the bedroom he'd shared with her with another woman stood out in her mind more than the bloody scene that ensued. This was a memory she was very clear about. She really didn't want to talk about Ben anymore.

"Hey, Boss, you got a phone call," Mitch said as he approached Neil with a cordless phone.

"Tell them I'm busy," Neil said in a tone that told Sabrina she was going to have to finish her story.

"Even if it's Faith Chase?" Mitch asked, eyebrows raised.

Neil placed his hands together as if in prayer. "Especially if it's Faith Chase."

Chapter Ten

Sabrina rushed away from Neil's office at Bar None, knowing Faith Chase had found out that she had discovered a murder victim. Somehow Chase had also determined that Neil Perry was representing her. While Sabrina was fully aware that the only thing that moved more quickly on an island than a thunderstorm was gossip, she was still stunned to find the media already involved. Neil had refused Chase's call but dodged when Sabrina had asked how Chase knew to call him.

Glad to be out of the tiny booth and out from under the microscope, Sabrina was surprised to feel fairly sober. She noticed Mara Bennett coming down the steep slope of the St. John Car Rental parking lot in her work boots, still wearing a tool belt.

Sabrina called over to Mara, who was probably on her way to meet the twins, Liam and Kelly, at the ferry. Although the kids were at least sixteen, Mara still insisted on meeting them at the dock every day when they arrived from St. Thomas, where they attended a private academy. Sabrina admired Mara's lioness style of mothering, perpetually poised to protect her cubs, though they were not hers biologically.

She looked at her friend and smiled. Mara Bennett wasn't a pretty woman. Petite with a plain face and unruly curly brown hair, her enormous brown eyes made her look interesting. Mara was solid and curvy, not hot and blonde like the women with whom her husband, Rory, cavorted. It was a funny thing, Sabrina thought. The more she grew to know and admire Mara, the prettier Mara became. Yet the more she knew the lecherous Rory, tanned with a full head of sun-kissed hair and embarrassingly blue eyes, the less attractive he grew.

"Hey, Mara," Sabrina called.

Mara converged with Sabrina on the sidewalk, falling into place with her.

"Sabrina, are you okay? I heard what happened out at Villa Mascarpone today. Awful, just unthinkable," Mara said.

Sabrina was grateful to hear Mara express concern about her.

"I'm okay. It was pretty grim, and I feel terrible about our guest."

"I can imagine. It's just too close to home, literally, and it's got Rory in a dither," Mara said.

Sabrina stopped and looked at Mara.

"The police are interviewing me again tomorrow. Faith Chase has already begun 'investigating' the case. Mara, I don't know if I can go through this again."

"Wait a minute, Sabrina. Who says you'll have to? You didn't shoot this guy, right?"

"Of course not."

"So that's the big difference, sweetie. Last time, you did shoot the guy. Oh, I know, there were good reasons. I'm just saying you're not going to be charged like you were in Nantucket. There will be nothing for the media to 'chase.'" Mara made little quotation marks with each hand. "What we all really should be concerned about is finding out who did do it."

"I know," Sabrina said, realizing she hadn't really considered this question. She had been too preoccupied by the thought she might be considered a "person of interest" to the police.

"Exactly. Even though the kids were safe at school over in St. Thomas all day, I can't wait to see them get off that ferry in a few minutes and give them big, fat hugs. I don't like that it was in our neighborhood," Mara said.

Of course Mara would be terrified to bring the kids home next to where a murder had occurred just hours before.

"Mara, you practically live in a fortress. You don't have to worry. You know that; you built it, for God's sake." Sabrina pictured the sprawling stone house Mara had built on the slope opposite Villa Mascarpone at the farthest point in Fish Bay when she and Rory had decided to get married. When Sabrina had first seen the house, Mara seemed almost embarrassed by its opulence. She explained Rory insisted it be luxurious and secure. He had told her you could never be too careful with children, particularly when you lived on the remote side of a tiny island. Mara confessed she had willingly agreed. She was so delighted to have children come with the deal that she said she would have carved a moat into the mountainside if he had asked. Sabrina remembered asking Mara about the name of the house. In Gaelic, Cairn Suantrai literally meant a "lullaby atop a mountain." They crossed the street where Henry was leaning against Sabrina's jeep.

"Hey, Henry," Mara called.

Henry jumped a little and looked at them as though he'd been caught ready to steal the car.

"What's with parking in a priest's parking space, Sabrina? Are you looking for more trouble?" he asked, hands on hips, facing his business partner and friend.

"Relax, Henry. Father Posada is in San Juan for a couple of days," Mara said. "Oh, here's the ferry." She waved good-bye as she hurried down the road toward the dock.

"Hop in. I'll drive you home," Henry said to Sabrina, opening the door to the driver's seat.

"No need. All of the vodka on the island couldn't get me drunk tonight. I'm fine to drive."

"Well, your head may be sober, but your blood is probably pretty pickled and you don't need any more trouble right now. Can you imagine how easy you would make it for the cops if they got you for a DUI right now?" Henry asked.

She didn't bother answering. She got into the passenger seat, and he asked how it went with the guests she had picked up.

"You do not want to know. Seriously. You would have thought they were booked at the White House and that I told them they were being switched to a Motel 6."

Henry pulled out of the parking space and started to slink through the narrow streets of Cruz Bay, past happy vacationers who were wandering from bar to bar after a full day in the sun.

"I finally had to tell them the villa was a crime scene," Sabrina said.

"They were that difficult? Even with all the perks we threw in?"

"It really didn't make sense to me, but nothing today has made sense from the moment I pulled into the driveway at Villa Mascarpone," Sabrina said.

"No, it hasn't. Has it occurred to you that the only one who seems to have been out by Villa Mascarpone today was Rory Eagan? I'm just saying."

"Oh, that wouldn't be good for Mara and the kids, would it? Speaking of not good, Faith Chase has found me." Henry understood better than anyone on St. John— well, except Neil Perry now—why she'd taken refuge on the island.

"I know. I saw her on television while I was at Bar None," he said. They began climbing up the road named Jacob's Ladder, although real islanders knew it as Genn Hill. Whatever you called it, it was as close to being vertical as a road could get. Sabrina had been terrified driving up or down it when she first moved to St. John. Now she loved it, like she loved the old wooden roller coaster in the amusement park back in Allerton.

"I'm in trouble, Henry. I know it," she said.

"Wait and see what Neil can do. You're just freaking out because of what happened in Nantucket, Sabrina. But this is different. You didn't have anything to do with Carter Johnson's death. There is a real killer out there. Once they find out who it is, then the focus will be off you. I get why you're panicking, but I think it will be okay."

They were winding through the curves on the road to Fish Bay. In the far distance on the last hill, Sabrina could see the glow of light, the kind she remembered hovered above shopping malls from when she lived in Boston. She had a sinking feeling in her chest, because she knew this halo hanging above the villa must be from lights being used by the police as they investigated the scene of the crime.

She couldn't see her own tiny house, which was tucked into a hillside, but she couldn't wait to get there. She'd missed her evening swim with Girlfriend at Hawksnest Beach, but she could take her for a little walk and then take a long shower and wash away the muck of the day.

"Can you pick me up in the morning around eight thirty?" Sabrina asked, remembering that she had to accompany Neil the next morning to meet with the police. Henry would need her jeep to get home. "I can drop you off to pick up the van when I meet Neil at Bar None."

"Quick, get down," Henry said, pushing her head forward and down with his right hand. Sabrina heard the panic in his voice and followed his instruction without question.

"Farther, duck down as far as you can go," he said, as he reached behind into the backseat and pulled the plastic trash bag filled with rags for cleaning into the front seat and threw it on top of Sabrina. Her head was jammed against the glove compartment and her knees were thrust between her breasts. She was not pleased.

"Henry," Sabrina said, in a plaintive tone.

"The INN TV van is parked about two hundred feet from your house. That wannabe reporter from Faith Chase is reporting on camera. She's pointing to your house. There are about six cops coming in and out of the house, some with bags. Girlfriend does not look happy."

"Get Girlfriend and let's get out of here. Please, Henry," she said.

Sabrina heard Henry get out of the jeep and the sound of the whistle she and Girlfriend knew so well. She heard him push the driver's seat forward and then the galloping sound of her beloved chocolate lab bounding down the dirt road.

"Good girl," he said, shutting the door and turning on the ignition simultaneously. Sabrina felt him hit reverse, backing the jeep to the side of the road and then moving forward with a tear.

"Hang on," he said, as the jeep accelerated even more.

Sabrina felt the bag of rags before she felt the impact of Girlfriend on top of them.

"Backseat, backseat," she heard Henry say as he pulled the dog off her.

He took a left onto the main road because there was nowhere to go if he went right, other than back to the scene of the crime where she had started this never-ending day.

Sabrina felt the plastic bag lifted off her and began to rise up from the floor.

"Are we being followed?" she asked, not wanting to look around and see for herself. She knew from experience that if she was caught by a camera, even in a moving automobile, that photo would be plastered on the Internet, newspapers, and, worst of all, the *Chasing Justice* show.

"No, but I wanted to make sure we got enough distance in case they tried. How the hell did they get someone down here from INN so fast?"

"They're like dust mites, Henry. They're everywhere. You just can't see them. Now I wish I hadn't talked you into putting 'Ten Villas' on every vehicle we own."

Sabrina had been reluctant to bring attention to herself when she'd moved to St. John. Henry had pointed out that, while that might work for Sabrina's personal life, it wouldn't for the business they hoped to build. Now in their gecko-green jeeps, they were like moving targets for INN, the "In" News Network.

"Should I take you to my place?" Henry asked.

"How about the Westin and you keep Girlfriend for the night?" Sabrina asked, doubting the hotel was pet friendly and not wanting to bother him any more than she already had. Their friendship originated in a common interest, which was to get away from horribly painful experiences they'd had in Boston and start over completely with what money they'd each been able to extract from their respective situations. Would her circumstances topple Henry's second chance for happiness? She hoped not. He might not have been tried for first-degree murder, but Allied Air had betrayed him as badly as Ben had her.

"Um, Sabrina, where do you think those reporters will be staying?"

Of course they would have to stay at the Westin, the only hotel on island other than the fabulous and famous Caneel Bay Resort, originally developed by one of the Rockefellers, which was always booked and probably wouldn't let some low-level INN reporter in its front door. It bothered Sabrina that she wasn't thinking clearly, and she was scared to realize how limited her choices could be on an island.

"Call Neil and tell him what's going on. I'm taking you to my condo," Henry said.

Sabrina turned her cell phone back on, having shut it off while talking to Neil at Bar None. She could see she had missed two calls. One from Angela Martino, the other from Sam Leonard. She didn't want to talk to either but figured she should at least listen to their messages. She put her phone on speaker so Henry could hear.

"Sabrina, how could you let this happen? I cannot believe blood has been spilled at my precious Villa Mascarpone. Do you think anyone is ever going to want to rent my villa ever again? You'd better call me and tell me how you are going to fix this situation. I consider you and Henry responsible. You should not be renting my villa to the kind of people who go and get themselves murdered." Click.

"Let me handle her. Don't give Miss Hissy a second thought," Henry said, and Sabrina decided to let him.

"Sabrina, it's Sam Leonard. I think we may have been a little hard on you today. You know, the messenger instead of the message. But Deirdre had her heart set on Villa Mascarpone. So I just want you to know that whenever it's released or whatever the police do when they finish up, we'd like to move right over there."

"Wow. That ought to help you with Angela," Sabrina said.

"Yes, and it gives me an idea," Henry said as he pulled into the drive for Trade Wind Estates, where his condo was located high atop Gifft Hill. He stopped at the imposing wrought-iron gate and hit a few keys. It swept open, letting them slip through. They'd be safe from INN, at least for tonight. Sabrina's relief was palpable.

"Call Neil," Henry reminded her.

She called Neil's cell phone. He'd given her the number before she left Bar None. He picked right up.

"What's up, Salty? You haven't gotten yourself in more trouble, have you?"

Sabrina knew he was trying to keep it light. Hearing his voice made her want to cry for some reason. Not just weep but bawl, preferably while he held her. She was close to the edge.

"Neil, I just thought you would want to know that you were apparently right. Judging from the number of cops at my house, it looks like they're conducting a search. They must have gotten the warrant."

"That's okay. They'll make a mess of your house, but that's the worst of it. You've got nothing to hide. Nantucket has nothing to do with this," he said. Sabrina felt encouraged by how positive he sounded.

"The other thing is, Neil, INN is on island. A reporter was outside my house when the cops were doing the search. They probably filmed Girlfriend as Henry rescued her," she said, sorry even her poor dog was being displaced by this sorry saga.

"Well, it looks like I finally have a costar I deserve. They got me on camera a little while ago when I threw their sorry asses out of Bar None," Neil said.

For the first time that day, Sabrina smiled.

Chapter Eleven

"Where are you?" Kelly tapped the text message onto the screen of her cell phone, stepping outside onto the deck surrounding the pool where reception was strongest. This was just one more reason she hated living on an island where nothing was easy. Even texting or talking to her boyfriend was a major hassle.

"In the cabana, inside the shower stall. Come see me," Seth texted back.

Seth had done this before, always when her father was out. Hidden in the cabana, he told her to sneak out for a short visit. Seth's daring nature thrilled Kelly more than it scared her. Making sure Mara wasn't in sight and that Liam was with her in the kitchen doing homework, she walked past the pool toward the end where the cabana stood. She opened the door slowly and quietly, slipping in and closing it again. She passed the shelves of pool toys and towels, moving to the corner of the cabana, and pulled the shower curtain open about six inches. Seth stood waiting for her with a huge grin on his face. He pulled her into his arms.

"Seth, we have to be careful. I'll never get out of the house again if we get caught," Kelly said, but she wasn't able to resist the strength of his embrace.

"Hey, wasn't I your pool guy long enough to get the lay of the land? I can disappear down the hillside in a flash. I've told you not to worry. We won't get caught."

"Did you hear what happened today?" Kelly asked, stepping back, putting a little distance between them.

"Hear what?" he asked.

"Someone died next door at the vacation villa today," she said.

"Really? At Villa Mascarpone? I hadn't heard," Seth said. "What happened? Someone drown in the pool? Have a heart attack?"

"I don't know what happened. There's a bunch of cops over there. Liam heard on the ferry someone carved out the guy's heart over a drug deal, but I don't believe it. You know how stories on the ferry grow."

"That brother of yours has quite the imagination," Seth said with a chuckle.

"He just gets carried away when something exciting happens. It gets his mind off of other things." It bothered Kelly that Seth considered her brother immature. Kelly wanted to explain that Liam was having a terrible time struggling about how to tell Mara he was gay. But Liam had made her promise to keep his secret and she would.

"I don't know what to believe about what's going on at Villa Mascarpone. All Mara will say is that the guy staying there died."

Kelly shifted so she could peek through the shower curtain and make sure Mara wasn't looking for her. She didn't think Mara really cared if she went out with Seth, but her father had gone ballistic the day he caught Seth flirting with her near the pool. Thank God he spent most nights at Bar None.

"Well, you know what you can believe, don't you, babe?" Seth cooed into her ear.

"No, tell me," she said, melting a little inside.

"How much I love you, sweetheart."

"How much, Seth?" she asked, wanting him to tell her how special she was to him and how what they had was nothing like what he'd ever shared with another girl, even though she was sure she wasn't his first. He was hers, though, and she knew they had something different.

"Babe, I wish I was better with words. When can I see you for more than a few minutes in a cabana? I want to—"

"Kelly, dinner's on," Mara called through the sliding screen door to the pool. Kelly was almost relieved she had to leave. It was one thing when she was alone with Seth in the dark and he was doing those things to her, but she wasn't quite comfortable when he talked about it.

"Coming, Mara," Kelly called out and then whispered to Seth, "Love you too, and soon isn't soon enough for me." She wished she could be with him tonight. She liked how he could take her away to a place entirely new to her. She just didn't like talking about it.

Chapter Twelve

Henry had just placed the frosted martini glass with three olives on the kitchen island in front of Sabrina when her cell phone rang.

"If that's Ms. Angela Hissy Missy calling to bitch about how we let a guest get murdered in her villa, don't answer," Henry said, pouring himself a glass of Pinot Grigio.

"No, it's Lyla Banks." Sabrina picked up the phone and answered. "Hi, Lyla."

"Sabrina, is that you? I'm always so surprised when someone knows it's me on the line. I forget about caller ID, even though it's my favorite modern innovation. How are you, dear? I wanted to make sure you are all right after the shock you had today."

Sabrina was touched by Lyla's concern. She felt her eyes begin to sting with tears. Here she was, a woman who had cried only a handful of times in her entire life, and in one day, she had come close to crying about a half-dozen times.

"I'm okay, Lyla. Really, I am. I'm at Henry's right now because the police and the media are swarming all over my cottage."

"Well, they must have imported some new police recruits because Villa Mascarpone is still crawling with cops. They have so many garish Klieg lights over there that Evan wasn't comfortable taking our nightly skinny-dip in the pool after dinner. It's really rather creepy," Lyla said.

Sabrina had to admit, skinny-dipping wasn't something she imagined as part of the Banks' daily routine, but she liked the idea. "Oh, Lyla, I should have thought to call and offer one of our empty villas for you and Evan. Tree Frog is available and close enough to Cruz Bay to make you feel a little more comfortable," Sabrina said, looking at Henry for approval. Henry nodded. They both knew how anything out of the Banks' ordinary routine threw Evan completely off, including bright lights flooding their side yard where the pool was located behind a hedge of Hibiscus.

"Oh, no, we're fine here, Sabrina, but thank you. It's just, well, you've seen how Evan is when something unexpected happens. And this was definitely unexpected. Do you know, when we lived in New York, we bought a gun, just in case someone broke into our apartment while we were there? We didn't care if we weren't home and they helped themselves to our stuff, but Evan said we shouldn't risk our own safety. We both took firearm training and have gun permits. Never had to use the gun in all those years, and yet now that we decide to retire to safety in St. John, we have a murder across the way. It's mind boggling," Lyla said.

"Oh, Lyla, I am sorry. They'll have this all sorted out soon, I'm sure. Do you feel safe out there? Do you still have the gun?" Sabrina asked. Henry's eyebrows arched upward at the word "gun."

"Yes, yes, we brought it with us. It's locked in the safe. Neither of us felt we needed it out. Do you think I should take it out and place in my nightstand? You know, just in case?"

Really? Put a gun in a nightstand next to your bed, just in case? Sabrina didn't think she was the person to answer that question.

"Lyla, you have to do whatever makes you and Evan feel safe and secure," she said, taking a sip of the smooth slippery martini before it got warm. Henry made the best martinis in the world and she deserved this one.

"I know, I know. I'm just rattled by how much this seems to be affecting Evan. I persuaded him to tuck in early with the new John Grisham book I snagged today while volunteering at the library. Evan loves Grisham's books, though he doesn't remember them very well anymore.'"

"Lyla, I'm sorry. Is there anything I can do?" Sabrina asked, knowing how difficult it was for Lyla to watch her husband of forty-odd years slipping away from her. It was such a cruel illness, for both the victim and his loved ones.

Lyla had explained to her one day that Alzheimer's disease resulted in what was called "ambiguous loss," which meant that the person who had the disease was gone, even though his body remained present. "How can you mourn a loss when you are sitting across the table on your lovely deck overlooking the Caribbean staring into his vacant eyes?" Lyla had asked.

"You already have, dear," Lyla said now. "You've listened."

"You call any time. All of this will be behind us by the time we meet for our book club next week," Sabrina said.

"I certainly hope so, dear, but in the meantime, I'll get the gun out of the safe and if I meet anyone who looks like or works for that horrible hack, Faith Chase, I'll give it to her between the eyes."

Sabrina clicked off her phone and took another sip of the Bombay Sapphire delight.

"I finally know who I want to be when I grow up, Henry."

"And who's that?"

"Lyla Banks."

Chapter Thirteen

Deirdre walked out of the master bathroom, tying the sash to her white gauzy cotton robe, wishing it weren't so short or transparent. She didn't want to remind Sam about what he was missing after he'd attempted to make love to her. She couldn't. She just couldn't. Didn't he know?

Sam sat on the edge of the huge mahogany four-post canopy bed, so high you had to climb on a stool to lie on. Deirdre watched his long, graceful feet dangling above the tile floor. A gentle breeze sneaked through the sliding screen doors. She knew he was thinking what a waste of a beautiful night in the Caribbean this was.

She climbed into the huge bed, leaving on her robe and nightie beneath. He lumbered onto his back. She waited a few minutes. Sam was still, but she knew from his breathing that he was awake.

"It's not a honeymoon, Sam. You know that," she said, her mouth in a pout Sam had once called beautiful.

"Deirdre, we're stuck, for lack of a better word, in a villa so opulent I couldn't have even imagined it. We're here until they clear Villa Mascarpone. Why can't you just go with it? Try to enjoy this as if it really were a vacation until we get over there."

"Because I am consumed. Consumed and confused. We were so close. What happened? What went wrong?"

Deirdre turned to him now as he lay back in bed, stark naked, just wanting what any man in bed with a lovely woman would want.

"How do I know? Neither of us expected him to die here. It's bizarre but probably totally irrelevant to us. It only complicates things, Deirdre. It doesn't necessarily change them," Sam said, reaching out to take her hand.

She curled her fingers around his and gave them a squeeze.

"I've waited so long, Sam. I've spent so much time and energy, not to mention nearly all the money Daddy left me. I can't help how I feel. And what are we supposed to do now?"

He rolled over and faced her. Deirdre knew he found her what he called "stunning in a fragile way." Wasn't that why she'd brought sheer white cotton lingerie, giving him the hint of what was beneath? He had been seduced by her subtlety, which was lost on most men. It certainly had been on her ex-husband.

Ever since Sam had seen her at a faculty meeting one fall in South Hadley, he had been devoted to her. He had heard the stories, even read some of the newspaper clippings. But it didn't matter. He was under a spell when it came to her.

"Honey, I was only trying to make love to you, make you feel better. I wasn't trying to upset you," Sam said, tracing his index finger under her chin.

"I know, I know. But you knew this about me when we got married. I can't do anything about it. You know I love you; it isn't about that."

Sam sighed.

Deirdre knew Sam appreciated that, for the most part, they had a good life, both of them now tenured professors at Mount Holyoke College. He taught history; she taught English. They had a beautiful home. They even had a golden retriever. But it wasn't enough. It just couldn't erase the past, give back what had been taken from her.

"Of course I do. Deirdre, I get it. I cannot imagine how I would feel in your shoes, especially now that I'm a father. I'm behind you, I just wish I could ease your pain, make this easier for you," he said.

"I hope I didn't ruin everything," Deirdre said in a voice as small as a child's.

"Nope. Don't even worry about that. I've got your back. I already left her a voicemail apologizing if we seemed insensitive when she told us. We were just tired and disappointed after a long trip."

Deirdre smiled. "You are brilliant, Professor Leonard. I think that will work just fine. Now if you could just figure out what we should do next."

"We move over to Villa Mascarpone as soon as it's available and take it from there." Sam kissed Deirdre's forehead, which got a little less wrinkled with the brush of his lips. He was so good at soothing her.

"Maybe there's something we could do before that," she said and rolled toward him.

Chapter Fourteen

Sabrina awoke to the familiar sound of a predawn tropical shower. Most mornings, St. John washed its beautiful face with a short rainfall just before sunrise. It was enough to quench the thirsty cisterns that collected rain for the island water supply but not so much to dash the plans of tourists. The sound of the rain was soothing, the green smell of wet vegetation intoxicating. As much as she had loved the challenge of forecasting the ever-changing weather in New England, Sabrina found great comfort in the predictability of the weather on St. John.

Girlfriend was planted next to her, lying against her butt, on top of the expensive multithread cotton sheets Henry had in his guest room. Sabrina was surprised by how well she had slept, collapsing into bed after a quick shower. She reminded herself about what Neil had said. There was no reason she shouldn't sleep well. She had done nothing other than to find a dead body. This wasn't Nantucket.

Sleep had restored her strong sense of logic. Because she was short on guidance, Sabrina had spent her whole life relying on her ability to think things through. Reclining on the guest bed, which was more comfortable than hers at the cottage, she took inventory of the events from yesterday. First, Carter Johnson had been fatally shot sometime before 10:35 a.m. when she'd arrived to clean the villa. Second, Evan and Lyla had not been home, nor had Mara and the children. Third, Rory Eagan had come out of his home to complain to the police in the afternoon, but how long had he been at home? Where had he been that morning?

No, this wasn't Nantucket, Sabrina saw. Neil was right. She didn't have to become a victim here. She had shot Ben, who was her husband. She had been arrested. Their personal relationship had provided the prosecutor with a motive. But she hadn't shot Carter, didn't really know him, and would make sure no one uncovered any information to the contrary.

Sabrina found her backpack on the chair where she had plopped it the night before and took out a black jersey tank dress, fresh underwear, and black flip-flops. She always kept these essentials packed to change into for her trips to the ferry when she met and greeted guests. Even though St. John was very casual, Henry had reminded her she needed to look the tropical version of professional for their guests. She owned six dresses identical to this one for just that purpose. After being dressed by the chic shops on

Newbury Street in Boston for television, Sabrina relished the simplicity of her wardrobe in St. John.

Her stomach growled, reminding her she had eaten only a handful of onion rings and conch fritters the day before. She found her way to Henry's sleek, stunning kitchen, which was done in black and white, as was every room in his condo.

"No more ambiguity or ambivalence for this guy," he'd told her. "I want to know where I stand. Black or white, no gray." Poor guy was still scarred by a man who had each foot in a different world and had decided not to join Henry's.

Sabrina opened the fridge, praying for leftovers. She wanted meatloaf, mashed potatoes, and macaroni and cheese. She wanted Ruth.

Staring at several containers of yogurt, she shut the door and rested her forehead against the cool stainless steel door. She still missed Ruth more than twenty years after her death. Sabrina wanted to be back in the diner, eating spaghetti and meatballs, her homework spread out on the table next to her plate, listening to thunder roar over the ocean in the distance. When she was growing up, all she could think about was getting out of Allerton. Now she dreamed of returning.

She was attempting to figure out how to use the European coffee maker, which required a three-credit course to understand, when Sabrina heard Henry behind her. Girlfriend's footsteps followed his.

"Here, let me do that," he said. She stepped aside and gave Girlfriend a pat. Sabrina found it funny that Girlfriend would sleep in some mornings after she'd gotten up. She admired her independence.

"Thanks," Sabrina said, noticing how Henry looked as crisp as white sheets hanging on a clothesline in pressed khaki shorts and a white T-shirt.

"Honey, you have to do something with that hair," he said, scooping coffee out of a bag he'd taken out of the freezer.

"I'll put it up, under a hat," she said defensively. She had planned to wear a big sunhat, under which she would tuck her black natural curls, and dark glasses when she went with Neil to the police station.

Henry took Girlfriend for a stroll while Sabrina fixed her hair. They decided Girlfriend should stay at Henry's today rather than go with them and draw attention. Sabrina wanted to avoid the media as much as possible.

Sabrina and Henry synced their phones, which Henry had charging on the counter with their laptops. They were joined at the hip electronically so that Ten Villas was as organized as you could be on an island where power outages were as common as morning showers.

"It's pool day," Sabrina said, looking at the calendar on her phone as she got into the car Henry had borrowed from one of his neighbor's villas. They would be far less visible in a vehicle that was not gaudy gecko green and without Ten Villas etched on its doors.

"Pool day!" they both said simultaneously. It was pool day, Sabrina realized, everywhere *except* for Villa Mascarpone, which was on a different schedule because their pool guy had done the Banks' pool across the road the day before. Seth should have done Villa Mascarpone yesterday.

"Do you think he went out there?" Sabrina asked Henry.

"I have no clue," he said.

"I didn't notice if the pool was done," Sabrina said, feeling like she had screwed up.

"Of course you didn't notice. You'd found a dead body, for goodness' sake."

"This complicates things," she said. She just wanted everything that had happened yesterday to be deleted with a simple push of a key.

"Well, maybe, but it may make things easier for you, Sabrina. You may not have been the last person to see Carter Johnson alive," Henry said.

Sabrina felt a rush of relief, followed by a short shot of shame. Their pool guy, Seth Larson, was really just a kid, probably in his early twenties. She shouldn't wish the police on him.

Henry drove to the back of Bar None and got out, letting Neil Perry into the driver's seat as they had prearranged. Neil looked over at Sabrina in her large brimmed straw hat trimmed with black ribbon and large sunglasses.

"Very Audrey Hepburn. I like."

"Our pool guy Seth Larson may have been at Villa Mascarpone yesterday morning," she said, not wanting to waste time during the two-block ride to the police station.

"Really?"

"I don't want to get him in trouble. He's just a kid," she added quickly. "And don't forget, Rory Eagan was just next door."

"It dilutes their theory, Salty. It doesn't mean the kid did anything. It just means they can't say you were the only one with the opportunity," he said, pulling into a parking lot for a small trucking company located behind the police station. They'd have to climb over a cinderblock fence to get to the back of the police station, but that was far more preferable to risking being seen entering the front door.

"I want you to say as little as possible when we're in the station. I wouldn't bring up this Seth business unless they ask about it. You don't want to sound desperate to pin it on someone else. That could make you sound guilty. Just tell them what we went over last night. You do remember last night, don't you?"

"Of course I remember," she said, sounding indignant. Arrogance must be a required course in law school, she decided, and Neil Perry had probably gotten an A. Sabrina noticed he had put on a shirt with a collar and some boat shoes for the occasion, which redeemed him a little.

Neil gave her a hand so she could follow him up over the three-foot wall onto the asphalt lot at the rear of the police station. Sabrina found the roughness of his hand on hers oddly comforting. She wasn't looking forward to being interviewed by Janquar.

They walked to the back door of the police station where Neil knocked three times. The door opened, and a young woman said, "Come in quick." Her nametag told them she was none other than Officer Detree, with whom Sabrina had spoken the day before.

Detree ushered them down a cool corridor into a windowless room with a table and six chairs. Sabrina could hear the hum of computers and printers in the background. The air conditioning was on so high that she wished she had a jacket.

Neil and Sabrina sat next to each other, waiting for Detective Janquar. She knew not to say anything private. He had warned her that cops often make witnesses wait so they can eavesdrop on conversations.

"So how'd you end up with your name, Salty?" Neil asked, filling the air.

"That's not my name and you know it."

"No, no. Sabrina. How'd you end up with a name like that?"

"It's from a movie," she said.

"Not the Hepburn and Bogie one?"

"Yes," she said. Neil was clearly trying to frustrate anyone who was waiting to hear her confess to Carter Johnson's murder.

"So why Sabrina?" he insisted.

"My father was my grandmother's driver. He and my mother eloped. That's why," Sabrina said, shivering a little in the frigid room. She never liked telling people about how her parents had such a romantic start because the ending was so disappointing. If her parents were an adorable old couple now recounting how she was named, it might be cute. But given that her mother had abandoned her father when she was a toddler, never to be seen or heard from again, the name Sabrina only underscored how ridiculous their relationship had been.

"Wait a minute. I thought you grew up poor," he said.

"I did. My grandmother disowned my mother after that. I've never met her," she said, wanting him to shut up. Apparently, Leon Janquar shared her view, entering the room seconds later, ending Neil's endless questions about her background.

"Sorry to keep you folks waiting," he said, filling the room with his bulk. He had a manila folder in his hands, which looked surprisingly full.

Neil rose and offered his hand.

"Good morning," he said.

Sabrina sat not speaking. Let them play games, she thought.

"So what have you brought me that might help us out here?" Janquar asked. Sabrina was surprised at his cordial tone.

She opened her backpack and slid out the Villa Mascarpone file, which was noticeably thinner than the one Janquar had.

Janquar flipped through the pages.

"This is it?"

"Yes," she said, wanting to scream, He was only renting a villa for two weeks, not buying it. Sabrina apparently pleased her lawyer with her brevity because Neil had a sweet smile on his face.

"Okay, let's go through what happened yesterday," Janquar said.

Sabrina repeated what she had told him yesterday, just as she had recounted the details to Neil. It sounded very reasonable to her. She had no connection to Carter Johnson.

When she was finished, Sabrina sat back against her seat as Neil leaned forward in his.

"Have you been able to locate his family?" he asked with a concerned, furrowed brow.

"No, his wallet was missing. The camera bag and backpack Ms. Salter remembers from his arrival are gone too. All that was left in the rental jeep was his duffle bag with his clothes in it." Janquar stood to signal the meeting was over.

"Ms. Salter, if you remember anything else, please let me know. Please do not leave the island without checking with me. You are at the very least a material witness in this ongoing investigation."

She wondered if she should tell him about the pool guy, even though Neil had suggested she wait. They still didn't know if Seth had even gotten out to Villa Mascarpone yesterday. Besides, Sabrina wanted to run out the door before Janquar changed his mind.

"Detective Janquar, you haven't mentioned the search warrant. We're aware you've been through my client's private residence. I assume there's a list of everything you removed and that you'll provide it to me, along with a copy of the warrant?" Neil asked, though it wasn't a question.

Janquar slid open the file once more and found several pieces of paper.

"These copies are for you, Counsel. Better use the back door. Ms. Salter's fans are gathered out front," he said to Neil as they shook hands. Sabrina knew he meant reporters. She was relieved although a bit mystified by Janquar's seeming disinterest in her.

As she exited the room, Sabrina saw Seth Larson coming down the hall with a broad grin across his face.

Chapter Fifteen

Henry hopped on his scooter and tore up the roads to Sabrina's house after dropping her off with Neil. He was worried about what might have gone on there during the search, what might be missing or, at best, tossed around. He had passed the police station on his way and confirmed what he suspected. The reporter he had seen last night at Sabrina's was standing out front, microphone in hand.

He climbed the hill leading to Sabrina's cottage, wondering if someone had been posted there from INN to observe any inane detail that might be used to titillate an audience, but the road was mercifully empty and quiet. All the action must be at the police station.

The house was locked with no external signs that the police had conducted a search. Inside, things looked a little sloppy, but no worse than he'd seen Sabrina leave it on occasion. The file cabinet drawers weren't closed fully and the desk looked a little disorganized, but otherwise everything was fairly normal. He began tidying up, and in a half hour, the house looked like it did most days.

Sabrina lived a little like a refugee, Henry thought. He knew she had grown up poor with only the essentials, but she had learned to live in luxury once she had become a weather anchor in Boston. He'd seen her on a number of flights, dressed casually but still managing to look elegant, tall, and graceful, although a bit skittish, like a bird being watched. Since they'd arrived on St. John, Sabrina shunned anything that would draw attention to her, dressing and decorating so generically that Henry found it painful to watch.

He picked up the landline, which was far more reliable than his mobile. First, he started down the list of people who had rented villas from them.

"Hello, it's Henry from Ten Villas. How are you? I'm sure you've heard the dreadful news about the murder here in St. John. What you may not know is that it took place in one of our houses. Totally unrelated to Ten Villas, of course, and probably drug related, but it's having the most unexpected effect. With all of the media attention, we are getting inquiries for reservations at a rate we can barely handle. So Sabrina and I have decided that it's only fair we call our loyal customers and give them a chance to confirm their reservations for next year with a credit card number and a deposit."

One after another, people thanked him and expressed sympathy that something so nefarious had happened on St. John. Some wanted details about the murder, but no one, absolutely not a one, wanted to cancel their reservation.

Henry chose to save the people who stayed at Villa Mascarpone for last. Here, he thought he might run into some opposition. But again, somewhat to his surprise, people clucked about how awful it was to have a murder at the villa where they stayed and then went on to ask if there were any physical signs a murder had taken place. Henry thought they were hoping for bullet holes in the wall. He didn't understand it, but people just gobbled up crime these days. He enjoyed a good true crime story himself, but much more when he was watching it on television.

He decided he would call the Kimballs, the couple who had originally cancelled their reservation at Villa Mascarpone, to see if they would be interested in reserving for next year. They had simply sent an e-mail when they cancelled, saying they understood they wouldn't lose their deposit because someone else would be renting the villa. Although Carter Johnson never said he was referred by the Kimballs, he called the same day for a last-minute booking, so Henry and Sabrina assumed he'd come through them.

The Kimballs, along with many of their clients, had previously rented directly from owners or from other agencies. Upon starting Ten Villas, Henry and Sabrina had worked very hard at convincing the owners of each villa that the services they performed not only would be worth the cut they took from the rental fee but also would please renters and persuade them to return season after season.

Henry dialed the number and was pleased when he was not sent to voicemail.

"Elaine," Henry said, as if he had reached an old college classmate he'd been trying to locate. "It's Henry from Ten Villas. How are you?"

Elaine answered politely that she was fine and thanked him again for returning the deposit.

"We hope your cancellation wasn't because you haven't been happy with Villa Mascarpone or Ten Villas."

"Why would you ever think that, Henry? John and I love Villa Mascarpone. We wish we had enough money to buy it. But you know why we didn't come. How could we resist?" Elaine asked.

"Resist what?" Henry asked, wondering what she was talking about. Had he missed an e-mail or something?

"The prize, Henry, that fabulous prize. I must say you and Sabrina are doing an amazing job marketing your business. We had such a good time."

"Well that's great, Elaine. Where did you go?" Henry asked, his brain starting to hurt from a puzzle he had no interest in. He just wanted to get Villa Mascarpone rented so he could call Angela Martino and get her off Sabrina's back—and his.

"Hawaii, Henry. The prize we won in the Ten Villas drawing. I mean, when Mr. Taylor called and told me, I just couldn't believe it. I thought it must be a scam. But sure enough, the tickets and reservations at those fabulous hotels arrived. I think John liked Kauai the best, but I really think Maui is nicer. Three weeks was unbelievably perfect. We just got back last night. I haven't even unpacked." Elaine spoke with a postvacation high in her voice, the one that lasts about twelve hours after you arrive home.

Mr. Taylor. Hawaii. Ten Villas drawing. What was Elaine Kimball on?

Henry took a deep breath and made a strategic decision. Whatever was going on, it was way too complicated to unravel on the phone with Elaine. He was over his head here.

"Well I'm glad you folks had a good time, Elaine. We've had a little incident down here at Villa Mascarpone. You probably missed it on the news, but a man was murdered there yesterday." Henry went on to explain that the result had been surprising. Ten Villas was swamped with rental requests. If the Kimballs were troubled by what happened, he had a list of others wanting the villa, especially for next year, on the anniversary of the murder. Did the Kimballs want to return next year during their normal month?

Of course they did. And they would have no trouble appearing in advertisements for Ten Villas and St. John claiming, "Better than Hawaii." They'd taken tons of photos, just like Mr. Taylor had instructed them to.

Henry hung up, confused and limp with exhaustion. He had one more call to make.

"Angela, Henry here. How are you?"

"How do you think I am? You and Sabrina have made my beautiful villa a haven for the underworld. What kind of people are you renting to anyway? And why weren't the Kimballs there? I've rented to them for years and no one got murdered. Who will ever want to stay at Villa Mascarpone ever again?" Angela wailed into the phone.

"Everyone who has rented in the past year, Angela. They're all coming back and have authorized deposits on their credit cards. I told them all that the notoriety of what's happened has everyone clamoring to come here and that Villa Mascarpone has become the place to be." Henry felt like he was back in the first-class cabin of Allied Air, sucking up to people he would never choose to be with.

"Oh, Henry, that was so clever. I'll feel so much more confident tonight during my interview. Thank you," Angela said.

"What interview?" Henry asked.

"I'm going to be on *Chasing Justice* with Faith Chase. I hope you'll watch."

"Wouldn't miss it for the world, Angela. Break a leg," Henry said and meant it.

Chapter Sixteen

Sabrina looked at her cell phone to see what time it was as the car peeled out of the parking lot. It was 10:00 a.m., not even twenty-four hours since she had found Carter Johnson on the hammock. How could her life have been changed so much in one day by a person she barely knew?

"Where are we going?" she asked, as Neil drove up the hills on Centerline Road, the main roadway that bisected the island from one end to another. Lush, green trees on each side of her, the sweet smell of the rain forest so thick she wanted to dive out of the car and hide in it.

"Somewhere we can talk without a cop or a reporter," Neil said in a tone too serious for her. Didn't he feel the relief she had when Detective Janquar released her after minimal questioning?

"Are you worried about Seth being at the police station?" Sabrina asked, realizing that she was. What worried her was the cocky expression Seth wore when she saw him in the hallway. She had always liked Seth, although after hiring him as their pool guy, she saw him very little. He went on his rounds cleaning pools for them and for other people without much fuss. Sabrina had no complaints from clients and only knew a little about him being fired by Rory Eagan, allegedly for trying to date his daughter.

"I'm worried about everything, Salty. That's what lawyers do and why I got out. Well, at least one of the reasons," Neil said as his cell phone began bleating "Ants Go Marching."

"Hey. Yeah, I know about it. I ordered it. Does it fully cover the front of her house?" Neil asked the caller. Sabrina wondered if he was talking about her house or maybe he had a girlfriend he was having work done for. She didn't like that idea.

"Well, then, great, it's working. She can park in it. It's big enough. Sure," Neil grunted into the phone, handing it to her. "It's Henry."

"Hi, how're things going?" Sabrina asked, knowing everything do to with Ten Villas was on Henry's overly full plate. He quickly let her know that he had soothed all their clients, that her house now had a forty-foot-long empty cargo container sitting in front of it, and that Villa Mascarpone was no longer being held captive by the police as a crime scene. It was more than she could absorb.

"A container? How did that happen?" Sabrina asked, remembering how much she and Henry had each longed for the one containing all their worldly goods to arrive in St. Thomas when they'd first moved to St. John. There was no choice about how to get your stuff to St. John. You either chucked it all or shipped it in a container. She and Henry had made a compromise. They'd each tossed about 75 percent of what they owned and thrown what they couldn't bear to leave behind in a container they shared. Now it seemed Sabrina had one all to herself.

"Ask your boyfriend," Henry said.

"He's not my—" She stopped midsentence, not wanting Neil to hear Henry tease her. "I guess I better go up to Villa Mascarpone and clean it up."

"That's where I'm headed. I told the Leonards they could get in by two o'clock," Henry said before hanging up.

Sabrina told Neil she needed to get to Villa Mascarpone. Although normally Henry could clean any villa by himself, as could she, leaving him with that puddle of dry blood and the vapors of death wasn't something she could do to him.

"Great, I need to see the place," Neil said. He pulled over at Tony's Kitchen, a roadside beverage and snack van, and got out. He came back with two opened cold bottles of Guinness and a bag of salt-and-vinegar potato chips. Sabrina took a gulp from her bottle and felt an explosion of flavor on her tongue.

"This is the best sip of beer I've ever had," she said, grabbing a chip out of the bag.

"That's the problem with beer, Salty. Nothing can ever taste as good as the first frosty sip. After that, it's all downhill."

"That's kind of a downer, Neil, especially considering you own a bar."

"It's reality. Speaking of which, it's time you get real with me. What's with that kid, Seth? Do you have any idea why he'd be at the police station? Does he know something about the guy at Villa Mascarpone you aren't sharing with me?"

Neil emptied his Guinness and then started the jeep and drove up Gifft Hill. They passed the fork in the road, which was a wooden fork painted fluorescent green decades before by some ex-patriot with a sense of humor, she'd been told. Sabrina's take on it was that if you lived in St. John, you'd already reached the fork in the road.

She told Neil what she knew about Seth. He was probably just a little over twenty-one and had come to St. John after dropping out of college. Seth told her he lived on a boat for a while, but he was too antsy to be confined in small quarters. The tiny apartment he now rented in Cruz Bay was no bigger, but it was on terra firma. He started the pool cleaning business, something he had learned while as a kid working in Florida. He had a thriving business within six months. If something went wrong, you could call him and he'd be out on the job within a half hour. Sabrina liked Seth. She just didn't like the way he'd looked at the police station.

Sabrina dodged the question about Carter Johnson.

"Tell me why I have a container sitting in front of my house, Neil," she said. Nothing made any sense to her, and she couldn't imagine how the placement of a container in front of her modest Caribbean cottage would unscramble her life.

Neil explained that the container he ordered be placed in front of her house was to protect her from the reporters. "Think of it as a barricade, Salty. A reporter embargo has been declared. No one will be able to see you once you park your car. Of course, you might have to run over one of them getting there, but no big loss."

They rounded the curve on the cliff leading to Villa Mascarpone. Sabrina wanted to jump out of the jeep, dreading the sight of the house, which previously had been her favorite on the entire island.

She felt better when she saw Henry's scooter parked in the circular driveway. He was already spilling bleach on the stone where the bloodstain sat like an ugly shadow. Neil pushed his sunglasses onto the top of his head without saying a word and did a 360-degree turn taking in the pool area.

"I'm going to have a good look around here while you two do whatever you do to clean a house. The cops have been here for twenty-four hours and probably taken anything of interest to them, but I want you both to be on the lookout for anything that seems different to you. Don't worry about how small it is, just let me know," Neil said.

Henry agreed to continue cleaning the stone pool deck and other outdoor areas, although Sabrina offered to help with the bloodstain. She was relieved when he declined and headed inside to do the interior. She started with the smaller bedrooms, which looked as though they had been unoccupied, and worked her way through the living room and dining rooms. She saw nothing different from the other times she had cleaned the house after guests.

Sabrina headed into the master bedroom, where she knew Carter Johnson had brought his luggage the day she picked him up at the ferry. Dirty sheets, to be expected, on the bed. Slightly damp towels lay on the bathroom floor and the smell of soap lingered in the air. But nothing unusual.

She picked up the linens, throwing them into a laundry bag, and made the bed with fresh sheets before moving into the kitchen. No messy pots and pans in the sink, telling her Carter had used the outdoor grill or eaten out, which she already knew. A few dirty glasses on the counter and a dishwasher filled with clean dishes. She opened the fridge and saw a few remnant bottles of beer and a nearly empty tray of a Ten Villas appetizer assortment, the kind they charged twenty-five bucks for, delivered. But Sabrina had never delivered any to him and knew Tanya hadn't either. Where had they come from?

Sabrina took the tray out of the refrigerator and walked through the kitchen into the dining area toward the sliding glass doors in the living room, where Neil was standing.

She called out to Henry across the pool, still slaving over the stain.

"Hey, Henry, you know anything about Carter Johnson getting a tray of assorted appetizers from us?"

"Maybe. What about the new bottle of propane next to the empty one I found on the deck? Do you know anything about that?" Henry asked, strutting toward her around the edge of the pool.

Sabrina stared at Henry but didn't answer. He met her eyes with equal obstinacy and silence.

"Well, whatever the hell the two of you know, you better clue me in right now," Neil said, "because you're playing a deadly game here. One or both of you could be charged with being an accessory to a murder if you are obstructing a police investigation by lying or even omitting information. And just to be clear here, I don't represent people who lie to me."

Chapter Seventeen

Neil's warning was a somber reminder of how high the stakes could climb when the police got involved in your life, a lesson Sabrina thought she had learned. She looked at Henry, her dearest friend, and was about to suggest they table the conversation for a more suitable time and place when she caught a glimpse of an apple-green object bobbing in the thick tropical shrubs that bordered the pool.

Sabrina placed her index finger against her lips, motioning to Henry and Neil to check out whatever it was she was seeing. Both crooked their necks and looked back at her in simultaneous curiosity. The bright-green object lent a sense of absurdity to the evolving saga.

Neil strode around the pool and stepped up over the small stone retaining wall onto the border shrubbery, moving through the thicket before disappearing into the brush. Sabrina and Henry remained poolside in silence, hearing only the rustling of bushes until Neil's voice boomed through the foliage.

"Hey, what do you think you're doing? This is private property. Get the hell out right now or I'm calling the cops."

"Sam, Sam. Come here quick," a woman said, with a tinge of hysteria in her voice.

The periwinkle-blue gate to the pool flew open and a very tall, middle-aged man carrying several pieces of designer luggage burst in, nearly falling into the hexagonal-shaped pool.

"Deirdre? Deirdre? Where are you?"

Sabrina raised both eyebrows, turning to look at Henry.

"Henry, meet Sam Leonard," she said.

"Then this must be Deirdre," Henry said, as the wispy strawberry blonde almost floated through the bushes ahead of Neil, her broad-brimmed green hat bouncing as she stepped over to meet Henry. She was a vision of delicacy, dressed in a long, gauzy pink cotton skirt and an ivory camisole. Sabrina found women who could pull off this look maddening. They managed without a word to inspire the men around them to take care of them, obviously a talent lost on her.

"Hello, Henry," she said, extending her hand to him as if she owned Villa Mascarpone and he were her guest. For a moment, Sabrina thought Henry might kiss Deirdre's hand.

"Thanks for getting us into our villa. We're very grateful, Sabrina," Deirdre said, apparently no longer feeling threatened by Neil. Sabrina accepted her handshake, not surprised to feel skin softer than a baby's bottom.

Neil stood behind Deirdre, just inside the gate, taking it all in. Deirdre turned and looked at him, as if she expected an explanation. Sabrina was surprised to hear Sam say, "And you're Neil Perry, aren't you?"

Sam walked over to shake Neil's hand.

"You know each other?" Henry asked, looking as confused as Sabrina felt.

"I don't think so," Neil said, "unless I met you at Bar None. I meet so many people—"

"No, no. I'm a history professor at Mount Holyoke. I teach an elective, the Great American Trial. The *State of California versus Rankin* is a big part of it, isn't it, Deirdre?" Sam said, looking over at his wife.

California v. Rankin? What was that all about? Two years of obsessing over whether she'd be convicted for her husband's murder had left Sabrina with little appetite for news about other cases. Now Sabrina wished she had followed the urge to Google Neil after that night on the beach to see what she had missed. Somehow, Googling him had felt like more of a commitment than she was prepared to make at the time.

"I would love to interview you for the course while I'm on the island," Sam said, in what Sabrina guessed was an academic's gush. This was just too bizarre.

Neil walked over to the empty propane container, like a man on a mission, and picked it up. "I'm afraid my lawyering days are over. I'm just a barkeeper now, and I like it that way." Sabrina had never seen Neil Perry so uncomfortable.

"Sorry if I frightened you on the path," Neil said to Deirdre, slipping through the gate.

"What path?" Sabrina asked, noticing Henry's furrowed brow. He was going to need Botox if this kept up.

"The one beyond the pool with such a lovely view of Reef Bay," Deirdre said.

There was no path beyond the pool.

Sabrina picked up the pail of cleaning materials and sack of dirty linens, smiled at Deirdre, and asked Henry if he was ready to leave the Leonards to enjoy Villa Mascarpone, especially since they had been so patient.

"You folks have a lovely stay," Henry said. "Oh, I'm sorry," he added. "You'd probably like a tour of the house." Sabrina could tell how flummoxed he was. Henry was normally the epitome of the gracious host, and he was off his game.

"No, no problem," Sam said. "We're fine exploring on our own."

"Well, the laundry room is on the lower level," Henry began to explain.

"I know. Carter told us," Sam said, looking over to Deirdre, whose smile resembled that of the mysterious Mona Lisa at the moment. The woman fascinated Sabrina, but what really caught her attention was hearing Sam use Carter Johnson's name.

"Carter told you about the laundry room?" Henry asked, his voice an octave higher than normal.

"We called the house number directly when you sent us the details about the location and contact information.

We had some specific questions. Carter called us back and filled us in. Such a sad end for him. He seemed like such a friendly man," Deirdre said, looking at her husband with the smile still on her face.

Henry and Sabrina filed out of the pool area through the gate without another word. Henry latched the gate behind him. Sabrina set down her pail and laundry bag. Without saying anything, they both walked over the driveway to the shrubbery that extended along the pool area.

There was a path, freshly cut, wide enough for a person to pass along, looking down at Mara Bennett's home and beyond to the splendor of Reef Bay with a sweeping view of Ram Head in the distance. Sabrina wondered if Carter Johnson had cut it so he could get a better view for his photographs.

They walked single file along the path until it ended at the edge of the Villa Mascarpone property line. In silence, they reversed direction.

Neil sat waiting in the car, windows up, air conditioning cranking. The sun was blazing down, although it was after 3:30. Henry walked by the car toward his scooter. Neil lowered the window on the driver's side.

"We need to finish our conversation. There are too many unanswered questions and too many coincidences for me. Homicide is serious and neither of you should take it lightly," Neil said as both Sabrina and Henry stopped in their footsteps.

"We'd better meet at my condo," Henry said. "It's the only place reporters can't get in. But first, I have to

meet the Gunnings at the ferry and take them out to Hibiscus Hill."

Sabrina had totally forgotten they had new guests arriving today. She really had left everything to Henry.

"Thanks, Henry. I'm sorry I'm so preoccupied with
what happened here. I'll make it up to you when this gets
straightened out. You can take some time off, promise.
I just don't quite have my wits about me," Sabrina said,
worried that forgetting details like new guests not only
arriving but needing to be picked up at the ferry might
mean her focus was off. When the cops were scrutiniz-
ing everything she did, Sabrina knew she needed to be on
her game.

Henry nodded and got onto his scooter. "If you get
there before me, make yourselves at home."

Sabrina and Henry had keys and knew the passwords and
codes to each other's houses. They had trusted each other
from the start, knowing neither of them could make it in
St. John alone after the trouble each had barely escaped. She
felt bad about the exchange they'd had about the appetizers
and propane. How important were those things anyway? It
was the trust that was important. They were going to have
to have a very difficult conversation for it to continue.

She got into Neil's jeep after placing the pail and laundry bag in the backseat next to the empty propane tank.
Neil looked as uncomfortable as she felt, his jaw drawn
tight, his fists clenched on the steering wheel.

"Can we go to Henry's and regroup?" she asked in a deliberately calm voice. She was not used to anything but an uberconfident Neil Perry and wasn't sure he wanted anything more to do with her and Henry. Sabrina realized she desperately wanted him to help her, and because she did not convey a woman in jeopardy as well as Deirdre Leonard, she might just have to ask him not to bail on her.

"Sure, Sabrina. Whatever you want," he said, pulling out of the driveway past the Bennett/Eagan home. Sabrina waved to Evan Banks as he leaned over a thick hibiscus hedge with a pair of pruning shears.

Chapter Eighteen

"Wait. Stop. Please," Sabrina said.

Neil applied the brake and looked over at her. His expression was so grim, Sabrina hesitated. But what she had to do would only take a moment. If she wanted to have friends, Sabrina knew she had to work at being one.

"I just need to check on Lyla. She called me last night upset about the murder."

"Whatever you say, Salty," Neil said, putting the jeep in reverse and pulling into the Banks' driveway next to their navy jeep.

"Do you want to come in with me?" she asked. Neil got out and came around to her side.

Evan was so intent on trimming the hibiscus hedge to perfection that he seemed oblivious to them. Sabrina had observed him tending to it on many occasions when she was out at Villa Mascarpone. She wondered if it made him feel accomplished, doing something physical when his mental acuity was diminishing.

Neil followed Sabrina in through the elaborate black wrought-iron gate, which divided the hedge into two sections. She knocked on the shiny coral door.

Sabrina wasn't prepared for the Lyla who opened the door. Lyla was what some people call "put together." Her short silvery hair always seemed combed into a feathery style. She frequently wore khaki shorts or skirts with crisp white cotton blouses. Lyla and Evan were both tall and lean, a handsome couple. No matter where you ran into them, they looked like they had just stepped out of an L.L. Bean catalog.

The Lyla who greeted them, unkempt, barefoot, and wrapped in a wrinkled blue paisley sarong, surprised Sabrina and made her feel embarrassed for both of them that she had decided to drop in and check on her unannounced.

"Lyla, I'm sorry. I should have called. We just finished cleaning up Villa Mascarpone and I thought I would check and see how you're doing."

"Oh, of course, dear. I know I look frightful, but please, please come in," Lyla said, putting her hands through her hair and straightening her sarong all at once.

Neil extended his hand to her.

"Mrs. Banks, I'm Neil Perry. I'm sorry we didn't meet properly yesterday under those unfortunate circumstances. I'm happy to meet you now." Neil gave Lyla a big smile. Sabrina appreciated what Neil was doing to put Lyla at ease.

Looking beyond Neil's handsome face, Sabrina realized that Lyla wasn't the only disheveled thing at the Banks' house. Sabrina had been to Lyla's house at least a dozen times since the couple moved from New York. Lyla's house was always as put together as she was. The open floor plan was inviting and casual. You could sit at the kitchen island sipping coffee and see the pool to your right. It was surrounded by a small tropical garden filled with bottlebrush trees; bougainvillea in shades of peach, fuchsia, and pink; Plumbago; and lipstick plants, all meticulously cared for. If you looked to the left, you could see the Great Room, as Lyla called it. The room was filled with wicker chairs and sofas with deep cushions covered in warm tropical prints and loads of throw pillows in case you wanted to take a nap instead of looking out through a wall of French doors that overlooked Fish Bay with St. Thomas in the distance. There were two bedrooms at the back of the home. Lyla had told Sabrina a one-floor home made sense at their age.

Today, the house looked like a burglary had taken place. There were cushions tossed here and there. Magazines and books Sabrina had seen stacked with almost mechanical precision were strewn all over the room. Sabrina could see into the kitchen that doors and cabinets were open everywhere.

"Lyla, what's happened? What's wrong?" Sabrina asked, knowing it had to be awful.

Lyla motioned for Neil and Sabrina to come into the kitchen. She pointed to the chairs at the island, the only clear place for anyone to sit from what Sabrina could see.

"He's lost the gun," she said very softly. "You remember, the gun I told you about last night on the phone. It's a

Colt Forty-Five. We had it in the safe, but when I went to get it, it wasn't there."

"Oh, god, Lyla, I'm sorry. But it has to be . . ." Sabrina looked around and realized Lyla had already come to the same conclusion. It had to be somewhere.

"Did you ask your husband if he put it somewhere, Lyla? I know he has some issues with his memory, but he must remember some things," Neil said gently.

"Of course. The good news is he remembered taking it out of the safe. 'A lot of good it would do us there, dear, if someone were to break in,' he told me. He was sure it was in the top drawer of his nightstand until he saw it wasn't. All he could say is, 'Don't worry, dear, it will turn up somewhere.' It will turn up somewhere. Right, just after there's been a murder across the way." Lyla was struggling not to cry, Sabrina could see.

"Do you think someone might have stolen it, Mrs. Banks?" Neil asked.

"Please, call me Lyla, Neil. I don't know if someone could have taken it. I try to stay one step ahead of Evan, really, I do. But his Alzheimer's is so fickle. Some days, he is just the old Evan, like this morning when he got up before me and made the coffee. But other days . . . I have to be careful not to upset him and remain calm, even if I am not. The disease is just so cruel to the victim and even more unfair to the people who love them. Damn Evan, anyway. Why couldn't he just have gotten a mild case of prostate cancer like most men his age?"

"Lyla, would you like Neil and me to look around? A second and third set of eyes? We'll only look inside so Evan won't see us." Sabrina looked over at Neil, who gave her a discreet nod.

"Would you? That way, at least I'll know it's not these aging eyes missing it. Do you know what a Colt Forty-Five looks like? Oh, that's silly. It doesn't matter even if you don't. It's the only gun we have in house," Lyla said.

A half hour later, no gun had been found, but the Banks' home had been restored to its typical order.

"Tell you what, Lyla. If you can get Evan out of the house tomorrow for a little while, I'll come back and search the shed and the yard," Neil said.

"Oh, thank you, I'd really appreciate that. Evan volunteers tomorrow at the park department while I help out with the Friends of the Library. We're gone almost the whole day on Tuesdays and Thursdays. There's a spare key under the rock below the birdbath."

"Are you sure you don't want to pack up and move over to one of our vacant houses for a day or two?" Sabrina asked Lyla.

"No, thank you for offering, but it would just throw Evan off his game and make him more confused. Familiar surroundings and routine are two essential elements I have to maintain. You are such a wonderful friend to offer and to come here to check on us, Sabrina," Lyla said, taking her hand and giving it a squeeze.

Sabrina shocked herself more than Lyla by throwing her arms around the older woman and giving her a hug.

Chapter Nineteen

If only all Ten Villa clients were as easy as the Gunnings, Henry thought, after leaving them at St. John Car Rental to pick up their vehicle. They had arrived from Wisconsin for their second stay at Hibiscus Hill, thankful to escape the brutal weather back home. They were grateful to Henry for his efforts, but they did not need an escort to their vacation villa.

Since he was already in Cruz Bay, he decided to run into St. John Spice, a shop filled with spices, coffees, and delectable smells of the island, which overlooked Cruz Bay and the ferry dock. He needed to pick up some coffee, which he noticed he was nearly out of when making Sabrina's in the morning. He climbed up the stone stairs to the second floor and nearly knocked Mara Bennett over when he pulled the door open. Mara was leaning over inspecting a dozen different kinds of cinnamon.

"Whoa, fancy meeting you here," he said. "What are you going to with that cinnamon—besides make your house smell terrific?" Henry knew Mara was one of the best bakers on the island. She had told him that the first time she met Liam, he had been filling his pockets with her spritz cookies at her Christmas open house. Henry couldn't blame the kid.

"Kelly and I are having a girls' night tonight, since Liam is staying in St. Thomas with friends. I'm making her my grilled French toast stuffed with cheddar cheese with fresh cinnamon and a sprinkle of nutmeg. She hated the idea of it when I first gave it to her, but once she took a bite, it became her favorite. She'll be on the next ferry," Mara said, looking at her watch.

Henry didn't bother to ask where Rory was or why he wasn't included.

"How about you? What brings you here?" Mara asked.

"Out of coffee. Neil Perry, Sabrina, and I are meeting at my house to discuss, ah, the situation," Henry said, feeling uncomfortable about not just the "situation" but the doubt it had cast on his relationship with Sabrina.

"How's she holding up? She seemed pretty sure the cops were going to think she was involved in what happened to that guy."

"Well, they've already gotten a search warrant and searched her cottage and made her go in to the station for an interview, so I think she has reason to be concerned," Henry said.

"I can appreciate Sabrina's concern, given her history, Henry. But this isn't anything like what happened on Nantucket."

They had walked over to the cashier, who was standing at a counter with a window behind it open to the beach at the rear. Above the counter, a medium-size flat screen showed what was going on at the beach just next to the dock. This was the view on the St. John Spice web cam, which had over twenty million views.

Mara pointed to the window and then looked up at the identical view on the screen.

"Oh my God. Oh my God," she said.

Henry looked out the window where he could see a young couple, sitting on the sand, shoulder to shoulder, staring off in the direction of the setting sun. The wind brushed the girl's soft blonde curls. The young man took a swig from a bottle of beer. Then the girl turned to do the same. They bent in and kissed, gently, almost innocently. But not quite so innocently, since Henry knew the girl was Kelly and the boy was Seth Larson.

"What do I do?" Mara asked Henry.

"This," Henry said to the clerk, pushing the power button off on the web cam next to the monitor. "Leave it off for the next ten minutes, please."

Before she could reply, he caught the sight of a man pacing in long, strong strides from Bar None on the left toward Kelly and Seth.

"Oh my God," Mara said, leaving her purchases with the confused clerk. Rory Eagan was headed toward the unsuspecting couple, and Mara and Henry both knew he meant business.

Mara flew down the stone staircase, which lead from St. John Spice to the walkway to the beach just feet away. Henry spilled down the stairs on her heels.

They arrived at the scene to find Seth standing, facing Rory. Kelly stood diminutively behind Seth. Henry glanced at the toppled brown bottle lying on the sand next to a green one, absurdly pleased to find that Kelly had been drinking a root beer while Seth seemed to favor Heineken.

Henry walked over, saying nothing, and stepped between Seth and Rory.

"I told you, you little lowlife, stay away from my daughter," Rory said to Seth over Henry's shoulder. He turned to face Henry, pointing his finger less than three inches from Henry's nose. "And you, you goddamn fairy, stay away from me and my family."

Henry remained silent, not moving an inch. He'd heard this before, countless times. He was impervious to Rory Eagan's ignorance.

"Rory, calm down. Henry is my friend. He's only here to help," Mara pleaded.

"Calm down, Mr. Eagan. I was just sitting on a public beach, having a conversation," Seth said.

"Don't tell me to calm down. You're a pedophile, taking advantage of a young girl. I warned you to stay away from my daughter," Rory said.

"Daddy, stop. Please." Kelly stepped forward.

"She's right, Rory. Knock it off," Mara said.

"We were just talking, Mara," Seth said, turning to her.

"I saw, Seth. I saw. You'd better be on your way," Mara said, her eyes never leaving her husband. Henry knew she didn't trust what Rory might do next. He was clearly buzzed, his face ruddy and eyes red.

"Go, Seth," Kelly said in almost a whisper.

"Come on, Kelly," Mara said, taking her stepdaughter by the arm, turning back to Rory. "You better go sober up and calm down before you come anywhere near home, Rory. I mean it."

"I'll wait with him while you ladies get to your car," Henry said, watching Mara and Kelly head toward St. John Car Rental, where Mara had parked.

"You people don't belong on this island, Henry. You and your partner," Rory hissed, but he didn't try to follow his wife and daughter.

Henry said nothing. Rory Eagan couldn't rile him. He had heard worse.

"I've told the cops everything I know. You'd better tell Sabrina, they're on to her. She won't get away with it this time." The sneer on Rory Eagan's handsome face made Henry wonder what he might be capable of.

Chapter Twenty

Once in the jeep, Kelly broke down and sobbed.

"I hate him," she said.

Mara didn't comment, afraid she might agree.

"I hate this island. I want to go home," Kelly continued. Mara had heard this before. Kelly had been complaining more frequently as she got older that there was nothing to do, no kids her age, no real life for a teen in St. John. "I want to go home" was a comment Kelly had been making when she was upset since Mara had met her.

Mara knew coming into the lives of a couple of kids who had lost their mother to a horrible car accident wouldn't be easy, so she signed up for what had turned out to be a decade of therapy with a woman on St. John who seemed to give pretty good advice. When Mara had asked her why Kelly kept saying she wanted to go home, Dr. Bell had explained she believed that Kelly was missing whatever life she had with her mother before she died, which made sense to Mara.

"Honey, you are home."

"I hate it here. I hate you," Kelly said, her nose running at a pace that rivaled her eyes.

Mara handed her a tissue before starting the jeep and pulling out of the parking lot.

"Stop it. I hate you. You're not my real mother," Kelly said, wiping her nose with her forearm, throwing the tissue back over to Mara.

They had been here before, but it still hurt. No matter how many skinned knees she bandaged, how many J.Crew catalogs she pored over with Kelly, how many essays she helped her write, Mara knew she would never—could never—replace the mother Kelly had lost. Inherent in her fierce love for Kelly and Liam was the cruel knowledge that it would never be enough. She feared Kelly wouldn't be able to have a healthy relationship with men after witnessing Rory's mistreatment of her. And Liam—Mara was pretty sure Liam was gay and could appreciate how much he must dread the day of reckoning when he revealed that to his father. Mara drew a deep breath and tackled the problem at hand.

"Kelly, I know I am not your real mother, honey. I get that there must be times when you miss her terribly and I'm sorry about that," Mara said, fighting back her own tears.

"Yeah? Well, she's dead. I know that. That's why I hate her, too. I hate you all, but especially Daddy. I wish he was dead, not her." Kelly slammed her fist on the armrest between them as Mara drove by what just yesterday had been the scene of a crime and now seemed serene compared to the tailspin erupting in her own car.

Chapter Twenty-One

Neil and Sabrina rode from the Banks' home in silence. Whatever annoyance Neil had expressed toward her and Henry before the Leonards arrived at Villa Mascarpone seemed to have been dissipated by Lyla's frantic desperation.

They turned on to Gifft Hill, climbing toward Henry's condo complex, when Henry came up from behind on the scooter and passed them. By the time they reached the gate, he had it unlocked, ready for their entrance.

Girlfriend greeted them at the door with such enthusiasm that Sabrina couldn't help but be energized. She bent down to feel the dog rush into her arms, her warm breath filling her ears. She closed her eyes as Girlfriend did what Sabrina had learned dogs did best: made it all go away.

She stood up and found Henry and Neil each seated in a white leather chair, opposite each other. Neither looked as if Girlfriend's magic had worked for them.

"Let me make some you something to eat," Sabrina said, liking the idea of having something to do in a room by herself.

"Knock yourself out, Salty. But after you've fortified us with some home cooking, we need to get down to business," Neil said, sinking more deeply into the chair.

"I'm not sure what you're going to be able to do with yogurt," Henry said. He had his legs stretched out before him and his eyes closed. "I tried to buy coffee when I was in town, but even that turned into a disaster. I'll tell you about it later."

Sabrina remembered yogurt was about all she had seen in the refrigerator that morning, but when she peeked inside, she found eggs, a chunk of cheddar cheese, and some Kerrygold Irish Butter in the dairy compartment. Sabrina loved that on a tiny island in the Caribbean, it was easier to find butter from Ireland than from Wisconsin. She opened the freezer and wasn't disappointed. Henry had the usual stash of bread most islanders keep frozen so it wouldn't mold in a day. On the shelf below was some frozen broccoli. Bingo, they were in business.

She let Girlfriend out through the screen door in the kitchen, which led to Henry's tiny yard. She always teased that it could be mowed with manicure scissors, but it was big enough to let the pooch do her business. Girlfriend came back in and flopped on the cool tile floor, happy to watch Sabrina cook, almost as if they were back home.

Sabrina threw the broccoli in the microwave to defrost and started beating some eggs, finding herself whipping them into a froth as she thought about Seth at the police station and those wacky Leonards at Villa Mascarpone. She wondered what was going on over at her place. She knew Henry had been able to secure the doors to her house. They had both been concerned that Tanya might stumble upon the INN crew, but Henry was able to reach Tanya by phone and divert her before she left for work. Sabrina couldn't imagine what the container looked like, barricading her place from the road. She wanted to be there, to sleep in her own bed, to be washing cleaning rags, baking appetizers, listening to Pavarotti, drinking vodka with lemons.

She tucked toast into the toaster and dropped a generous chunk of butter onto Henry's Cuisinart French griddle. He had such pretty stuff, and it always looked new, although she knew he cooked. The smell of the melting butter made her realize how ravenous she was.

"Smells good, Salty. You got a beer out there?"

"I'll get it," Henry said.

Sabrina checked the freezer, again pleased to see her pal Henry had her covered. Grey Goose, just where it always was. Just for her. She did love Henry, although she didn't like him not trusting her.

Ice cubes and a large splash of the Goose. Alas, no lemons, but otherwise, Sabrina was content to be sipping as she was stirring and spreading, not even noticing Henry had come for the beers. She could hear the television in the distance and wondered if the three of them could enjoy their omelets and pretend this was just another night in paradise. Sabrina plated the three cheddar broccoli omelets, placing triangles of toast alongside, each dripping with melted butter. She grabbed utensils and napkins and headed for the living room.

The sight of Angela Martino staring at her would have landed Girlfriend a triple omelet if Henry hadn't grabbed the plates from Sabrina. Angela looked heavier on Henry's mega flat-screen television, and her makeup seemed more professional, but there was no mistaking that jowly, scowling expression and those small, dark, shuttered eyes peering over a long, narrow nose. Sabrina had met her in person only a few times but knew there couldn't be two people in the world who looked so uninviting.

"What's Angela—" Sabrina started to say, when the unmistakably menacing sneer of Faith Chase spread across the screen. Her blonde helmet-head hairstyle curtained her face, in the middle of which sat a patrician nose with nostrils so flared a bird could fly in.

"Now, Ms. Martino, you say you've had this company—what do you call it? Ten Villas? Anyway, this company's been managing your home on St. John for how long?"

Angela's face reappeared. Sabrina wasn't sure which was worse. It wasn't a pretty choice.

"About two years, Faith. I had someone else before, but this new company approached me and offered some added services for my guests, so I signed on." Angela's typical bellow had diminished to a mere murmur when answering Chase's questions.

"And you didn't know you were hiring a woman who had been on trial for killing her husband, the father of two young children, did you, dear?" The sweetness to Chase's voice was thicker than Karo syrup. Sabrina hated Karo syrup.

Sabrina stumbled over a chair. Neil pulled her down next to him and put his arm around her. Sabrina let him.

"No, of course not. I live in Chicago. That case apparently was in Boston. I had no idea. And Sabrina Salter never volunteered that information," Angela said, throwing Sabrina under the INN bus as she looked down, away from the camera, as if forlorn.

"What a piece of work," Henry said, downing the end of his beer. Henry never chugged beer.

"Tell me, dear, do you have any concerns that the woman you hired to manage the villa you so love—the woman who killed her own husband, the woman who found a dead man at your beloved villa—do you have any concerns that Sabrina Salter might be responsible for that man's death?"

Neil squeezed Sabrina's shoulder. Her body was as rigid as stuffed game hanging over a fireplace. Was there any limit to what this woman would do? She was purposely distorting what had happened in the past to fit what she wanted people to think had happened now. Sabrina had no chance if the Faith Chases of the world got to write the rules.

"No, I really don't, Faith."

Sabrina felt oddly grateful to Angela for not agreeing that Sabrina was responsible for Carter Johnson's death.

"I mean, I should have been told about her past," Angela continued, "but I think I'm a pretty good judge of character, having run my cheese business, Martino's Wholesale Cheese Company on Commercial Street, for twenty-three years. Here in Chicago, we make the finest cheeses in the country, specializing in mascarpone, which is why I named my villa Villa Mascarpone," Angela said. But Faith Chase wasn't going to let this turn into a commercial.

"Thanks for speaking with us, dear. We do hope the family of your murdered guest can be found soon," Faith said, and Angela mercifully disappeared off the screen.

Henry hit the mute button on the television. The three beautiful omelets sat on his coffee table. Sabrina fidgeted, beginning to feel funny she was sitting so close to Neil.

"I will never get away from that woman," she said finally.

"Then you have to beat her at her own game, Salty," Neil said, standing and picking up the omelets before handing them to Henry.

"How do you do that?" Henry asked, sounding almost as bleak as Sabrina.

"Well, first we heat up these kick-ass omelets and make another drink to bolster ourselves. Then we sit down and figure out how to find who the real killer is."

Chapter Twenty-Two

Sabrina was impressed when Henry returned the reheated omelets along with cloth napkins. Even with the drama of the day, he remembered to garnish the plates with a curled peel from an orange he must have had stashed somewhere.

"So who's going first?" Neil asked. It was time to come clean about what they knew about Carter Johnson.

Sabrina took a bite of her omelet in an effort to avoid the answer, although it stuck in her throat like a chunk of dread.

"Oh, why not? I will," Henry said, sitting down next to her on the leather couch. Sabrina just kept chewing.

"One night I went to Skinny Legs to get a burger after checking some guests into one our houses over in Coral Bay. I didn't see anyone I knew, so I sat on a stool at the bar, ordered a Dos Equis, and started looking up at the television. The Red Sox were playing, losing bad, and I shook my head. A guy sitting at the stool around the corner of the bar looked at me and said, 'Those bums never seem to get it right, do they?' He had a New York accent and he didn't seem to be with anyone.

"I told him I was originally from Boston and that the Sox managed to break my heart every year, but usually not until September, after they'd made me think that somehow this year was going to be different," Henry said, picking up a bite of omelet with his fork but putting it down before he got it in his mouth. He wasn't looking at either Neil or Sabrina, both of whom stayed silent.

"I thought he was gay. I'm usually pretty good about getting a sense of this, and when I asked him where he was from and he told me New York, we had the usual Red Sox/Yankee banter and I thought he was flirting. Then I found out he was in one of our houses, and I thought, *Am I going to get lucky here?*

"He got up to leave, and I asked if he'd ordered our Ten Villas special appetizers, the kind we deliver to customers, and I told him Sabrina's famous for them. He said he hadn't and now he kind regretted it because he wasn't much of a cook. The next afternoon, right before the sunset, I went over to Villa Mascarpone with a complimentary tray of apps. I was all dolled up and arrived to find Carter out by the pool, taking photos with a telephoto lens of Ram Head in the distance. He told me he was a professional photographer, and he looked annoyed, not pleased, about me dropping by. I told him I'd just put them in the kitchen because I could tell I wasn't welcome. Carter ran ahead of me and started scooping up photos he'd taken, large ones, off the dining room table as I headed for the kitchen. I walked over to the table and told him I'd love to see his work, and he said he'd e-mail photos of St. John to me and Sabrina after he got home. Then he took the tray from me, put it on the kitchen counter, said thanks, and looked over at the door. I know when I'm getting the bum's rush, so I left. I felt like an idiot."

"Did you get to see the photos?" Neil asked as Sabrina put her arm around Henry, knowing that the miserable pilot who broke his heart had taken every ounce of confidence Henry had earned the hard way.

"I'm sorry," she said.

Henry squeezed her hand.

"You just didn't call it right, Henry. Everybody screws up once in a while. I see that all of the time at Bar None," Neil said.

"I was afraid if I volunteered that I had visited Carter to the police, they'd think I was somehow involved in his death. I saw what happened to Sabrina and I was afraid," Henry said. "But I did see a few of the photos. They were all taken from up at Villa Mascarpone. None at the beach or even in Cruz Bay. I'm pretty sure there were pictures of all of the surrounding houses up there. Oh, and I saw a picture of Mara and the kids and one of Mr. Banks. He got some nice shots."

Sabrina was remembering a conversation she was trying hard to forget when Neil turned to her.

"Okay, Salty. Your turn," Neil said.

"All I did was bring him a replacement tank of propane when he called and told me he had forgotten to turn the grill off. He said he was a city boy and never grilled before and probably never would again, given the way his steak turned out. I barely spoke to him, but I was afraid the cops would never believe me," Sabrina said, picking up her plate and then grabbing Neil's and Henry's, taking them into the kitchen where she would be out of their vision, where they couldn't see how pale she knew she had become. She'd felt the blood drain from her face as she told lie after lie. How could she tell either of them she had brought the propane to the house and then had an afternoon of wanton sex with a man she barely knew—a man who ended up dead two days later? Sabrina was having trouble enough admitting it to herself.

"Salty, get back in here. You have to see this," Neil called to her from the living room where the television was blaring.

"What?" Sabrina said, glad the topic of Carter Johnson was over, at least for the moment.

When she entered the room, Sabrina could see Faith Chase on the corner of the television screen superimposed over what looked like the beach next to the dock in Cruz Bay where another female reporter stood, mike in hand, fielding Chase's questions.

"So this is where Sabrina Salter has been hiding since she stood trial for killing her husband in Nantucket? She gets away with murder and then gets to live in paradise?"

"That's right, Faith. We've learned that Salter has her own business on the island, and we've reported from her home where the police recently conducted a search. The police aren't commenting on what they found, but I can tell you they took multiple bags of evidence," the reporter said in an exaggerated deep tone.

"Well, we're staying on this story, folks. With another dead body at her feet, dead from a gunshot wound to the abdomen just like her husband, let's see if Sabrina Salter gets away with murder a second time. St. John is one of the three U.S. Virgin Islands, what some people call 'Love City.' Well, it's not too lovey lately, is it? We're just learning that this tiny Caribbean island may not be paradise after all." Faith Chase signed off.

Neil grabbed the remote control and hit mute.

"I cannot stand the sound of that woman's voice," he said in a tone more serious than Sabrina could remember hearing before.

"Now she's attacking the whole island," Henry said.

But what Sabrina couldn't get past was hearing Faith Chase draw the similarities between Carter's death and Ben's. Her suggestion hung silently in the air along with the knowledge that if anyone ever discovered she had had an afternoon with Carter Johnson, Sabrina was as good as convicted. She was going to have to live with this secret until she died, or else it might kill her.

Chapter Twenty-Three

Deirdre knew how ridiculous she and Sam would appear if anyone could see them. They were sitting on the bar stools, which Sam had dragged from the kitchen out to the tiny trail bordering the pool. She sat on one, draped in long sleeves and a billowing skirt that protected her from the sun and the no-see-um insects. It was hardly happy hour for them, but she had an odd sense of satisfaction and destiny perched on her stool, sipping the crisp glass of Sauvignon Blanc Sam had poured her.

He sat over on his own stool, in Bermuda shorts and a T-shirt, already tanned and annoyingly oblivious to the bugs. Between them, a third stool had been placed for the bowl of pretzels Sam had supplied for their adventure.

The sun would set soon, and the chance to observe any neighborhood activity would disappear with it. Deirdre tried to hold off her growing fear of disappointment. She had waited so long; it was hard not to be impatient. She feared she might become impulsive if she didn't see something soon.

The little trail was cramped but still the perfect sur-veillance spot, just as he had described. The photos he had e-mailed were accurate, but it wasn't the same as actually see-ing Villa Mascarpone and its view of the villa below, which to Deirdre seemed a little like a fortress, with its heavy garage doors at the bottom of a downhill driveway. She'd seen the woman drive in and open those doors with a remote control.

"We'll have to go in soon, Deirdre. It's getting dark and the bugs must be getting you," Sam said, offering her his hand, which she took while never looking away from the road leading to the house where the children lived.

"I'm fine, honey. Let's give it a little more time. Pour us another glass of wine, and after we're finished, I'll go in," Deirdre said, squeezing his hand with affection.

"We've got time to do this right, you know." Sam filled her glass and then his. He amazed her, sometimes, when he could fill an ordinary moment with elegance. You'd have thought they were sipping champagne on deck chairs on the Queen Mary.

"Strange to encounter Neil Perry here, wasn't it?" she said, knowing Neil was a topic that would distract Sam from wanting to save her from the no-see-ums.

"Well, yes and no. I'd read he'd left California after his son's death. Finding him on an island where everyone seems to be running away from something isn't shocking."

"Such a shame—he saved Jess Rankin only to lose his own son," Deidre agreed, remembering articles about the brilliant defense Neil Perry had waged on behalf of a seventeen-year-old kid with Asperger's syndrome, accused of burning down his own house with his bipolar mother in a wheelchair inside.

"Well, Neil became such a celebrity. It wasn't really surprising the press would scrutinize his personal life. I don't think anyone knew his own kid had Asperger's until Neil's ex-wife gave an interview. It wasn't long after that the kid overdosed. Neil's defense of Rankin was so passionate that he was compared to Atticus Finch, which is why my students love studying the case," Sam said. He was a history professor with a law degree, which Deirdre sometimes suspected he regretted not using.

The sound of tires grinding on gravel in the distance made Deirdre sit at attention. She reached for her binoculars, the high-powered ones she'd bought on the Internet from the site that had been recommended. They were pricey, but it seemed silly to cut corners when the vision she hoped to see was one she'd spent more than a decade waiting for. They were tiny, almost like opera glasses, and added to the irony of the evening.

Deirdre turned on her stool so she could see the car as it rounded the corner, driving past the home of the older couple who lived across the street where a cruiser had been parked when Sam and she had first gone out to the path to sit and wait. It was gone now, so that she could see right inside the passenger side of the approaching car.

Deirdre's first sight of one of the Eagan twins was that of Kelly's face contorted in sobs. The girl seemed to be in agony. Deirdre looked toward the backseat to see if Liam was in the same state, but it was empty. Mara Bennett stared ahead, driving her vehicle down into the dungeon of a garage before Deirdre had a chance to think.

"Oh my god, Sam. Something is wrong, terribly wrong," Deirdre cried, turning to her husband who had been looking with the house binoculars.

"What? I couldn't see inside the car."

"Kelly's crying hysterically and Liam isn't in the car. Oh, dear God, Sam, you don't think something has happened to Liam, do you? Do you think he might be hurt or even worse? Oh my God," Deirdre said, her entire body trembling as Sam rushed over to hold her.

"Of course not, honey. It's probably just a teenage snit or something," Sam said, taking her into his arms.

Deirdre pushed free.

"We don't know that, Sam. It could be something terrible. I have to go. I have to."

"Deirdre, no. Don't. You've waited this long. Don't do this. You could ruin everything, honey. Please, please listen to me."

"I can't, Sam. I just can't. If it's a mistake, it's mine to make. I have to go," Deirdre said as she rushed down the path into the falling darkness.

Chapter Twenty-Four

Henry had just finished describing the fiasco on the beach in Cruz Bay when Sabrina heard her cell phone blast Kenny Chesney's "Way Down Here," her favorite St. John song and her ringtone. She decided she would just check who the caller was and then let it go to voicemail. Was there any one left on God's green planet who hadn't had a turn to harangue her today?

Lyla Banks was calling. As much empathy as Sabrina felt for the older woman, she had nothing left to give. Still, Lyla epitomized the courage, generosity, and grace Sabrina wished she could muster. If it were Sabrina calling Lyla, there was no question what Lyla would do.

"Lyla, how are you?" Sabrina asked as Henry and Neil both rolled their eyes. She knew they were cooked, too. It had been a long day, one that just didn't seem to want to quit.

"Well, all right, I guess. Listen, I don't mean to bother you so late, but I don't have Neil's number and I wondered if you could get a message to him for me, dear?" Lyla asked. Sabrina thought she sounded deliberately calm.

"No problem, Lyla. He's right here. Do you want to talk to him?" Sabrina said, knowing she was throwing Neil under the bus. He looked exhausted. He'd been dealing with people problems since first thing that morning when they'd gone to the police station together. Maybe that was why he'd left the practice of law and bought a bar. He got sick of needy people.

"No, that won't be necessary. I just wanted to let him know he won't have to come out to our property tomorrow to search for the gun, but I wanted to thank him anyway. It's all set. The property's been searched and no gun was found," Lyla said, a slight tremble finding its way into her words.

"Wait a minute. Who searched for the gun?"

Neil immediately perked up from the chair he was slouched in.

"Who searched for a gun where?"

Within three minutes, Neil and Sabrina were driving Henry's neighbor's car to the Banks' home with Girlfriend in the backseat. Sabrina admired how Neil hadn't hesitated when he heard the police had searched the Banks' residence. They parked, jumped out, leaving Girlfriend in the car, and approached the house.

Lyla opened the front door before they knocked and led them into the kitchen.

"Thank you for coming. I've given Evan a little sedative and he's asleep, thank goodness. He was so upset," Lyla said, choking up.

"Start at the beginning, Lyla, please. How do you know the police were looking for a gun?" Neil asked.

"Well, they didn't say exactly that they were searching for a gun, but the search warrant they handed me did, among other things. They found nothing. No gun, no backpack, no bag. But they rummaged through every nook and cranny of our home in the process of it. I feel violated. It was so degrading."

"Lyla, why would the police want to search your property?" Sabrina asked.

"Because Seth Larson told them he'd seen Evan at our house that morning, you know, when you found that man shot at the villa. Detective Janquar said when someone lies during a police investigation, it immediately makes them a suspect, a 'person of interest.' My Evan, 'a person of interest.' We should have stayed in New York."

Sabrina hoped Janquar never found out she hadn't disclosed everything or she'd be on the same list with Evan. She wondered why Seth would tell Janquar he'd seen Evan. Had Evan been home and not volunteering at the National Park?

"Lyla, didn't you tell Janquar where Evan was that morning? We all saw you both come home together that afternoon," Sabrina said.

"Of course. I was indignant. But Evan mumbled when Janquar asked him directly if he'd been here. Evan got flustered and said he suffers a little from memory loss." Sabrina thought now Lyla sounded angry. At Seth or Janquar? Or even at poor Evan? Or maybe all three?

"Janquar told me I could check with Glenn Dawson," Lyla continued, "who coordinates the volunteers at the National Park Service. Then they searched every inch of our home, shed, and yard. Evan's a mess. He needs constancy and predictability, not people in uniforms crawling through his garden and combing through his underwear drawer."

"Lyla, I'm sorry," Sabrina said.

"Did you talk to Mr. Dawson?" Neil asked.

"I did call him. It was humiliating for both me and even more so for Evan. Glenn told me Evan had forgotten his park department volunteer identification badge. Apparently Homeland Security issued some really tough regulations after Nine-Eleven and one of them requires volunteers to display a badge."

"Did Glenn drive Evan home to get his badge?" Sabrina knew that Lyla had always driven the pair ever since they were married, whether in Manhattan, Rome, or St. John.

"No, no, unfortunately. Evan had Glenn drive him to the library where he drove our car home to get his badge. Evan always carries a set of car keys in case I can't find mine, which is more often than I like to admit. This is such a mess," Lyla said.

"Well, as long as Evan still has a driver's license, there's no crime in him driving," Neil said.

"And he does, thank God. Not that he's ever used it much."

"You can't think Evan would do anything to hurt someone," Sabrina said, trying to rein Lyla in. She had to feel so alone and scared.

"Of course not. I know Evan better than I know myself. That man hasn't a violent bone in his body. I heard a couple of the cops talking while they were rummaging through my kitchen drawers. They're saying the dead man was using a fake name and was probably connected to someone here, Sabrina, so I think it will work out. They'll find their killer. But still, if someone used that gun, which is technically registered in Evan's name, could we be in trouble, Neil? I don't know whether to let the police know it's missing or just hope they don't find out we had it," Lyla said.

"I think you should consider volunteering that information to Detective Janquar, Lyla," said Neil. "It will be worse if they find you own a gun and then can't produce it."

"The cops think Carter Johnson was connected to someone here? What did they mean by that?" Sabrina asked. Seth had seen Evan the day of the murder. Had someone seen her the afternoon she visited Carter Johnson? It could only have been that fisher cat, Rory Eagan, sleeping all day, hunting at night.

"I really don't know. I'm finding this so exhausting," Lyla said.

"We'll let you get some rest," Neil said, tugging on Sabrina's arm, signaling it was time for them to exit.

Lyla hugged Sabrina and Neil, thanking them for coming.

"Oh, one last thing, Sabrina. When you get a chance, I'd love the name of another pool man," Lyla said, before closing the door.

Chapter Twenty-Five

Deirdre paused at the top of the driveway leading to the villa, noticing for the first time the sign on the stone house. "Cairn Suantrai" was carved in gold against a mahogany slab. Deirdre knew it was Gaelic, having been raised in Boston in a very Irish Catholic family. She'd taught plenty of Yeats and Joyce but she wasn't sure what "Suantrai" meant. A cairn was a mound of stones, and, certainly, that's what this house was.

She felt an urgency draw her toward the front door, but she knew she had to have a reason for coming to the house. She'd prepared for the situation by reading the thick "house book" provided by Ten Villas, which was a three-ring binder stuffed with information about the house, the island, and, most importantly, contact information for neighbors if there was an emergency. Mara Bennett was that person, listed on the front cover of the house book. There was no mention of her husband, Rory Eagan.

Deirdre took a deep breath and knocked on the door with confidence. She knew exactly what to say. She could hear movement but couldn't see into the house through the stained glass panes on either side of the heavy mahogany door. She thought she could hear wailing in the background. Or was it just her imagination? Feeling a little calmer than she had when the car with the hysterical girl inside had whizzed by, Deirdre decided that if something terrible had happened, Mara would probably be crying too. No, this seemed to be about Kelly. Deirdre expected that Rory wasn't home, although she couldn't be certain because the driveway led down into the garage on a lower level and was opened remotely, as she had observed. But the report had indicated that Rory was almost never home in the evening and could most often be found on a particular stool he seemed to favor at Bar None.

The door opened and Deirdre immediately heard the sound of crying—not hysterical but steady and weary. Mara Bennett stared up at her with curious, warm brown eyes. She wasn't a pretty woman, but in bare feet and khaki shorts and a white T-shirt, she had a certain island appeal, looking very healthy and natural. While not heavy, Mara was solid and looked strong.

"May I help you?" Mara asked, as Deirdre wondered if she looked as crazy as she felt. She had waited years for this moment and now it was reduced to a game of charades.

"I'm, we're, my husband and I are staying across the road at Villa Mascarpone and the power keeps flickering on and off. The house book Sabrina and Henry left said we should check with you to see if you were having the same problem, so they'd know whether it was a problem limited to our villa or perhaps a power company issue."

The soft crying in the background escalated to a full howl, followed by a staccato of sobbing.

"Is everything all right?" Deirdre asked, not able to help herself.

Mara opened the door for Deirdre to come in. Once inside the large circular hall with a terra cotta tiled floor and exquisite stonewalls dotted with shells and old wine bottles, Mara extended her hand.

"I'm Mara Bennett and that sound is my stepdaughter crying because two men adore her, so please, don't be worried. We should all have that problem, right?"

"I guess," Deirdre said, feeling stupid for not realizing that hardly anyone would tell a complete stranger about an intimate family discord. She could see she had overreacted, just as Sam had tried to suggest before she went off on a lark, threatening to ruin all their plans.

"I've only been home a few minutes, but I haven't noticed the power flickering. Let me peek at the clock on the stove. That's how I can always tell if the power's been off. What did you say your name was?" Mara didn't wait for an answer as she slipped through an arched doorway in the hall and disappeared, returning thirty seconds later.

"No, looks like we haven't lost power lately. But, you know, on an island, surges happen all the time and can be really spotty, affecting one house but not the one next door. You may want to give Sabrina or Henry a call. It could have to do with the investigation. You know about that, don't you?" Mara asked, giving Deirdre a tentative glance.

"Yes, we do. You're thinking maybe the police flipped some switches or did something to cause the circuits to flutter?"

"Well, it makes sense, if any of what happened over there makes sense. Are you okay staying there? I mean, if you're trying to get some relaxation during your vacation . . ."

Deirdre wasn't expecting to like Mara Bennett, but she did. There was a genuine kindness in her concern for her and Sam, even though she had her hands full with a bawling teenager. Deirdre felt a rush of feelings she hated having, her heart heading north and south all at once.

"We're fine, really. Sabrina and Henry offered us the villa we were in last night for our entire trip. We just had our heart set on this location. Thank you. I'm sorry to—"

Deirdre felt her heart begin to pound at the sight of the lanky and lovely young woman who appeared through the kitchen door, wearing the shortest of shorts, her long strawberry locks spilling down her back. Deirdre could see Kelly had dancer's legs with shapely calves running into tapered ankles.

"Where do you think you are going?" Mara asked, seeming to forget Deirdre's presence. No, this was about more than boyfriend trouble, Deirdre could see.

"I refuse to deal with that poor excuse for a father when he gets home. I won't put up with his BS," Kelly said, no longer crying and filled with resolve.

"What? Are you crazy? There's a murderer on this island, for God's sake. You can't go out at dusk the day after someone's been murdered two hundred feet away from your house," Deirdre said, surprised by her own outburst.

Kelly pivoted and turned away from Mara and seemed to notice Deirdre for the first time.

Before either could say a word, Deirdre said, "I'm sorry. I don't know where that came from. Probably thinking about what I'd say to my own daughter back home. I'll give you two some privacy. Thanks for the help, Mara. It was nice to meet you." Deirdre drew back through the hall and fled through the door. She'd risked too much with this insane interlude.

Chapter Twenty-Six

When Sabrina was a child, she'd dreamed about "normal." She wanted to be normal, to come from a normal family with siblings and a drooling dog, and to grow up to live a normal adult life. She wanted to get married, have some kids of her own, buy a raised ranch, and complain about taxes. Ruth used to tell her normal wasn't all it was cracked up to be, but Sabrina had been willing to give it a shot.

Tonight, Sabrina wanted her version of normal back. She wanted to return to her cottage and have a normal night's sleep in her normal bed with her dog curled up against her. She wanted the island she now called home to return to normal, the television crews and cameras to leave, and, most of all, she wanted Faith Chase to leave her and everyone else on St. John alone.

"Please take me home," she said to Neil when they got in the car.

"What?" Neil asked, as if Sabrina had said she wanted to go to Dubai to go shopping. "You can't do that."

"I need to go home. I need to find normal," Sabrina said.

"Look, Salty, I know it's been a rough couple of days and you're probably feeling it more than we are, but if you go up to that cottage of yours, Faith Chase and her vipers will be crawling all over you and your house," Neil said.

"I don't care. I want to things to be normal again," Sabrina said, whining like a child. "I just want my lousy little life back. I didn't ask for any of this."

She saw Neil's face wrinkle around the eyebrows with worry, worry that she was losing it.

"Look, you want normal, Salty? Let's take your dog for a swim. You swim every night with her, don't you?" Neil asked.

"What are you, crazy? A reporter will probably see us, and how normal will that make me feel?" Sabrina parked at Hawksnest Beach every night to take a swim with her dog because it was so accessible and had a little light in the parking lot. They would swim the short distance over to Gibney Beach and back. It was great exercise for them both, but especially for a dog on an island where it was often just too hot to take a decent walk. Sabrina loved their nightly swim, the routine of it, going home and showering in the outdoor shower with Girlfriend, and then sitting on the porch while her hair dried.

Neil took his cell phone out of his pocket and tapped a few numbers on the screen.

"Hey, Mitch, is Fred Sinkhole at the bar tonight? Good, let me talk to him." Neil said, pulling over to the side of the road, which seemed like a good idea to Sabrina since the road ran along a steep cliff. Sabrina listened, a little amazed at Neil and how easily he took command and shifted with circumstances, something she was not very good at.

"All set. Got a suit, Salty? I assume the dog doesn't need one," Neil said, tucking his phone back into his pocket.

"Of course, I've always got a suit in my backpack. But how are you going to make sure no one sees us?" she asked, not confident about Neil's plan, whatever it was.

"You can throw it on when we get there. Let's go. Timing is of the essence, like the lawyers like to say." Sabrina noticed he didn't include himself as one of them. She checked her backpack to be certain the drab one-piece black bathing suit was there. She was a little excited about getting her swim in. She loved looking up at the clouds and the stars at night. The constellations looked like the pictures in her school textbooks when she'd learned all about the world of weather. She felt safe in the water, swimming at night, away from the chaos human beings invoke upon each other.

They headed off with Girlfriend in the backseat sticking her nose out the window, clearly very excited about going somewhere with a much happier Sabrina.

"How long have you done this, Salty? Since you got the dog?" Neil asked as they descended the curvy steep hills through Fish Bay and Chocolate Hole and made their way through Cruz Bay, which was awash with nightlife: people walking around, couples arm in arm, normal, just like Sabrina wanted to be but had never been—and would never be, she now knew.

"Longer than that. Ruth, the woman who raised me, told me when I started kindergarten that you have to check out the weather in order to know how to dress. Early one morning, before I'd started school for the day, she caught me crossing the street in my nightie to go over to the beach. 'What in the blazes are you doing, honey?' she'd asked. I told her I was just checking out the weather like she had told me to. She roared laughing over that, but we had to negotiate my early morning trips to the beach. By the time I was in fourth grade, I was swimming every morning at six o'clock from mid-April to mid-October," Sabrina said, knowing she was babbling, something she tended to do on the rare occasions when she shared her personal life.

"So that's how you got to be a weather girl," Neil said.

"Meteorologist, Neil, not weather girl."

They passed the parking lot to Hawksnest, which confused her, but she stayed silent. As they approached Gibney, with its imposing gate, Neil slowed down.

"Fred Sinkhole told me it's open. There's a senior party down at the clubhouse in the morning, so they left it closed but unlocked," Neil said, looking over at her with a little smile that said, "How clever am I?" Fred Sinkhole worked for the park department when he wasn't on a stool at Bar None. His real name was Fred Cincola, and he was from Florida, but nicknames just seemed to stick on an island.

Neil opened the gate and drove down the short steep hill to the beach. Sabrina could smell rotting vegetation and hear tree frogs, but it was so dark that she couldn't see anything. At the bottom of the hill, Neil looked over at her and then back at Girlfriend.

"Throw on your suit, Salty. I won't look. Then you two can go on in and have your swim over to Hawksnest and back. It'll do you some good to change up your routine, get out of a rut, and do it in reverse. I'm going to jump in and float 'til you're back. Wake me if I fall asleep."

Girlfriend and Sabrina were in the water in seconds. It was still silky and warm from a day filled with sunshine and was lit by the moon peeking from behind a few clouds. Girlfriend paddled next to Sabrina as she stretched her arms in front of her, cutting through the water. She got lost in the moment as she moved her legs and arms, breathed, and then rolled her face into the water. Everything was erased but the sound and sensation of water all around her, and she was free. They reached the empty shore at Hawksnest and got out of the water for just a few seconds, long enough for Sabrina to take a few gulps of air and feel the pounding of her heart. She called for Girlfriend and they jumped back into the ocean, beginning their lap back over to Gibney where Neil was waiting.

Neil understood how much she needed to have at least a small piece of her life back tonight. He was lying on his back, floating, as he'd promised, his eyes closed, not a wrinkle near his brows. His long feet and toes had a white glow under the moonlight.

"Hey, we're back," Sabrina said. He turned, smiled, and reached over for her hand.

"Well, good. I've got towels I found in your backpack waiting for both of you up on the sand."

They began walking out of the water, still holding hands—Sabrina wasn't sure why, although she knew she liked it—when they were flooded by headlights nearby. Once she could focus, Sabrina saw the camera, the Faith Chase wannabe standing on the beach with a microphone in her hand, and a man to her left holding a light, which was shining on her. The INN van was parked next to their car. Girlfriend began barking and charging, while Neil resorted to his usual lawyerly eloquence.

"Hey, you assholes," he shouted as he blocked the camera with one of the beach towels he had picked up. He pulled Sabrina along as he called Girlfriend, tucking them into the car in seconds. Neil jumped into the driver's seat, gunned the engine, and zoomed up to the top of the hill before the reporter and crew could even get their equipment back into the van.

At the gate, he jumped out and swung it shut, taking the padlock Fred had left unlocked for the seniors and slamming it closed. An engine down the hill roared, headlights beginning to shine upon the hill.

"Come on, Salty. Let me take you and Girlfriend home. Looks like it's going to be safe there for the rest of the night after all."

Chapter Twenty-Seven

Henry welcomed the quiet after the rapid departure of Neil, Sabrina, and Girlfriend. He rinsed the plates Sabrina had left in his sink and placed them in the dishwasher. He was always amazed at how Sabrina could whip up a simple meal with just a few ingredients but also concoct a complicated gourmet recipe for their guests with ease. She always credited Ruth with her culinary skills, but Henry suspected Ruth never made crab and asparagus puff pillows or figs stuffed with almonds and Cabrales cheese.

The silence in the kitchen, with just the occasional humming of the refrigerator, was soothing to Henry after the blaring news on television. So much had happened in just two days. He felt he had little control over his newly created life. At least he could keep his own little world tidy, he thought as he grabbed the window cleaner and some paper towels and headed to the living room.

He sprayed window cleaner onto the glass table, wiping off the smudges from dinner.

The lone lamp cast a warm glow over the order Henry restored to his living room as he contemplated soaking in the hot tub or just calling it a night and flopping into bed. Before he could decide, he heard the sound of his doorbell. He found himself hoping it wasn't Sabrina and Neil. Though he loved her dearly and hoped her visit with Lyla had gone well, what they both needed right now was a little space from each other. He walked to the door, remembering how uncomfortable it had been revealing his mistaken impression about Carter Johnson being interested in him and listening to Sabrina admit to delivering a propane tank to Villa Mascarpone. He didn't think bringing a full propane tank to a guest was the big deal Sabrina made it out to be. Henry had a feeling Sabrina was holding back.

He peeked through the peephole in the front door to see a dark image with a gold emblem. Henry knew at once it was the police, probably with a search warrant. They must have come directly from the Banks' home. He opened the door to see Detective Janquar standing with a smile and Lucy Detree by his side.

"Mr. Whitman, I'm Detective Janquar."

"I know, Detective. We've met. Just yesterday. At Villa Mascarpone. What can I do for you?" Henry asked, wanting to appear cooperative and calm, neither of which he felt.

"You know we are investigating the murder of your guest, Carter Johnson. I have search warrant for your condo. I'll ask you to cooperate and let us in now." Janquar stepped over the threshold, not waiting for an invitation.

Henry accepted the document Janquar handed him. It looked official enough and was filled with more legal jargon than he had the energy to read, but he could see they were looking for evidence of any communication with the "victim."

Henry sighed and stepped aside so Lucy Detree and two other officers he hadn't seen behind her could enter. He so wanted to go to bed. The day had seemed endless. What did they want from him?

"Is there anything special you're looking for? I'm happy to cooperate, Detective. I have nothing to hide," Henry said as the officers donned purple gloves, which looked like they had been designed for Barney, and whipped plastic bags out of a larger black bag one of the officers had placed on the hall floor.

"I'll need to see your computers, any electronic equipment you use for your business," Janquar said, his voice and girth filling the hallway.

Henry knew that on the kitchen island, in plain view, sat both Sabrina's and his laptops, charging away, while his iPhone sat in his pocket. He knew there was nothing on either that could hurt them. He and Sabrina lived pretty boring personal lives and there was nothing salacious about their business, other than this little murder at one of their villas. But if Janquar seized the phones and computers, they were out of business. They had opted to forego a desktop computer and were modernly mobile in their choice of devices.

"Can you look at them here? If you take them, we won't be able to tell which guests are coming and going or be able to field inquiries about new business," he said, leading Janquar into the kitchen, which still smelled of melted butter and window cleaner.

"Nope, the laptops have to come to the station where our expert can take a look at them. I'll make sure he gets them back to you ASAP, but they're coming with me," Janquar said, as he unplugged Sabrina's from the charger and began winding wires.

"Detective, this puts us out of business. I don't suppose that would be the point, would it?" Henry asked, having had just about as much as he could swallow. If the cops really were this antagonistic toward Sabrina and wanted her to go away, whether off to prison or just off island, shutting down Ten Villas' communications was a good way to accomplish it.

"Mr. Whitman, we're investigating the death of a man who was a guest at one of your villas. Otherwise, we're not interested in your business, as long as you run it clean and legal." Janquar finished packing up Henry's computer as Officer Detree entered the kitchen.

"We're all set, sir. No files or paperwork. Nothing of interest. We didn't find any cell phones," she said.

"Mr. Whitman?"

"Sorry, I must have left it in the van," Henry lied. They were not going to leave him without his cell phone. He didn't care if that meant lying.

"Really? Isn't it an important part of your business communications, Mr. Whitman?" Janquar said in a mocking tone.

"Yes, but everything is all screwed up since Mr. Johnson's death. I'll bring it to you when I get the van."

"First thing tomorrow morning, Mr. Whitman. You can sit and wait for the laptops. And one more thing, Henry, if you don't mind me calling you by your first name. Listen, if you know something that would be helpful to our investigation, you had better disclose it. I know Ms. Salter is your partner and friend, but protecting her will only come back to bite you."

Henry gulped but didn't reply.

They were gone as fast as they had come. Henry looked at the empty counter and was furious. They'd even taken the chargers. He wondered if he should call Neil but felt too weary to recount what had happened. He was thinking about making a drink to calm his nerves when his cell phone tucked in his shorts pocket vibrated. He looked at the number, didn't recognize it, and wondered if Janquar was testing him to see if he really had the phone. His house phone began to ring. The caller ID showed the same number that had just come up on his cell phone. It didn't start with 340, so Henry knew it wasn't local. It looked like a cell phone number. Probably someone calling about a villa after having a few drinks and fantasizing with her boyfriend about a vacation in paradise. He and Sabrina had learned early on that some of their best customers were people who drunk dialed Ten Villas pledging to come for a vacation. They always made sure to get credit card numbers during the call.

"Ten Villas. This is Henry. How may I help you?" Henry said into the receiver, willing it not to be the cops or anyone else who would complicate his already overly complicated life. He and Sabrina had worked hard to build Ten Villas, and he wasn't going to let anyone dismantle it without a fight.

"Henry, I'm so glad I reached you. Whatever is going on down there? Are you all right?"

Henry collapsed onto his onyx leather couch, clutching the phone in his hand, not responding to the only man he knew he would ever really love.

Chapter Twenty-Eight

Sabrina shivered as Neil raced up Jacob's Ladder, heading for Fish Bay. He reached over and turned up the heat in the car, something she had never seen done on St. John. He had called Fred Sinkhole to tell him he should ignore any calls about some tourists being locked behind the gates at Gibney, which Fred, already fairly oblivious, was happy to do, especially when Neil told him his tab for the night was on the house.

Sabrina was thrilled about going home with her dog and, if she was honest, with this man she found endearing and adorable in an annoying kind of way. Neil was playful and funny, which she found very sexy, although she had seen he could have a serious, pensive side.

The vision of the unsightly container plopped in front of her cottage disarmed Sabrina, even in the dark under moonlight scattered through clouds. She got that it was a quick and brilliant improvisation that barricaded her from the carnivorous paparazzi, but it was still a little scary knowing she warranted protection to this extreme. Neil surprised her when instead of going around the container, he took a sharp turn onto a ramp and into it. He slammed on the brakes, making Girlfriend lurch toward the front seat, stopping just before hitting a parked motorbike.

Sabrina knew it wasn't Henry's because his was bright canary yellow. This color was too dark to distinguish, but it definitely wasn't yellow. Was some unflappable reporter hiding in the container, which was designed to protect her from the press? Girlfriend began barking, sounding as indignant as Sabrina felt.

"Stay here," Neil said as he started to slip out of the driver's seat.

"The hell I will," Sabrina said, getting out of the passenger's seat, Girlfriend right behind her. She realized she was barefoot, wet, and still in her bathing suit, but she didn't care. She wanted to know who was invading her house, her little piece of the world; she was ready to throw any intruder out on his or her ass.

Sabrina saw Seth Larson standing in the dim light of her porch as they approached. He was tall and slender, a graceful-looking young man, leaning casually against a porch pillar. Someone, a female, judging by the long bare legs, was sitting in Sabrina's wicker rocking chair.

Neil stepped in front of her, preempting any confrontation he probably thought was about to erupt, but Sabrina's irritation had morphed into acute curiosity.

"Sabrina, Neil," Seth said, extending his hand. Kelly remained seated behind him, looking a little sullen. Maybe Kelly still hadn't gotten over that nasty exchange between her father and Seth that Henry had mentioned. Sabrina was shivering, a little more than weary of the invasion into her world.

"Excuse me," Sabrina said, slipping past them through the front door, Girlfriend in tow. She passed quickly through the living area, noting nothing looked in obvious disarray, although the room didn't look quite like she lived there. She entered the bedroom, half-expecting to see her bed linens tangled in knots after the police search, but it was properly made. The way the pillows were propped, she knew it was the work of Henry, who must have put order to her cottage after the police search.

She grabbed the soft jersey T-shirt and pants she reserved for the cooler season and changed in the stall of her outdoor shower, not feeling as if her bedroom was private anymore. She could hear Seth through the window telling Neil he was sorry to be on the porch without permission, but it had been kind of an emergency, with Rory Eagan being out of control and Kelly needing to get away from him. When Seth had heard about the container blockading the house, he figured it was the best place to take Kelly.

Seth told Neil he had learned about the container from Tanya when he ran into her at a bar. Tanya had complained about not being able to work at Sabrina's cottage. Sabrina felt bad, knowing how meagerly Tanya lived in St. John, camping on friends' couches, sometimes even sleeping in her decrepit jeep, until she could afford a room of her own. Sabrina hoped Tanya understood. The trickle down from Carter Johnson's death seemed endless.

Sabrina went back onto the porch, not even bothering to put a comb through her hair. Why should she? These weren't guests. She wasn't having a party, a little porch get-together, was she? Something she never had because, why would she? Although, recently, Lyla had suggested Sabrina might host the reading group.

Neil and Seth were now seated on two of the other wicker chairs, which were gathered around a glass coffee table with a potted hibiscus on it. Kelly remained perched on Sabrina's rocking chair, her "spot," and Sabrina resented it and her, even though she knew Kelly was just a kid with a son of a bitch of a father. She knew she should have a little more empathy for Kelly, and she probably would have any other day. But not tonight.

"All right, what's going on here?" Sabrina asked, taking the last of the wicker chairs.

"It's my fault. Blame me. I just didn't know where to bring Kelly so she'd have a chance to regroup," Seth said.

Sabrina nodded without responding and noticed Neil remained silent. Sabrina was leery of Seth, knowing he had snitched on poor Evan.

"Kelly's dad is really angry and she needed to get out of her house for a while, so she walked Fish Bay Road to the—"

Sabrina turned to Kelly without thinking.

"You went out into the night alone in a neighborhood where there has been a murder? What, are you crazy?" she said, the words slipping out before she was aware they were coming.

"Great. Now I have a third mother," Kelly said, leaning forward in the rocker.

"What are you talking about?" Sabrina asked, really not needing any more mystery in the evening.

"Some woman you rented Villa Mascarpone to. She was over at the house talking to Mara and flipped out when I said I was going out."

Deirdre was over to see Mara? Why, Sabrina wondered and hoped something wasn't wrong at Villa Mascarpone; she didn't have the energy to cope with it and felt pretty certain Henry was just as spent.

"Look, honey, we know you must be pretty upset. After a falling out with your father in public, I can see why you needed space," Neil said with a tenderness Sabrina found touching.

"It was so embarrassing," Kelly said, her porcelain complexion becoming paler under the dim porch light.

"It's all my fault. I shouldn't have asked you to take an earlier ferry and meet me," Seth said. He sounded so contrite, mature, and responsible, but something didn't feel right to Sabrina.

"Does Mara know where you are?" Sabrina asked, realizing how frantic she must be if she didn't. The silence Sabrina got in response to her question gave her the answer.

"Either you call her or I will."

Kelly's face softened.

"I feel bad, leaving Mara alone with my father—that is, if he bothered coming home. Liam is in St. Thomas for the night at a swim meet. He hates being home. But I couldn't stand to listen to my father lecture me on why I can't see Seth when everyone on this island knows what he . . ."

Neil and Sabrina exchanged glances. Yes, everyone knew what Rory Eagan did because he made no effort to spare anyone the knowledge—an added level of insult for his family to bear.

"But I don't want to go back. Not tonight," Kelly said.

Sabrina watched Kelly, trying to imagine what it was like for her to balance all of the broken pieces of her young life. Sabrina knew how hard it was to have a drunken father. Oh, maybe hers had been poor and had better reasons to drink, but still either way, a drunken father could rob your youth, especially if you didn't have a mother. Oh, she'd had Ruth, and Kelly had Mara, but no one could ever fill the vast black empty hole where your mother was supposed to be. Although, Ruth had come close.

The September night was humid and the air was fragrant with the smell of the ocean. Ruth had come out the back door of the diner to dump some trash. When she looked up and spotted Sabrina, barefoot in her cotton nightie, perched on the mansard roof of the Victorian mansion converted into a boarding house where Sabrina lived with her father, Ruth slowed but didn't startle.

"What are you doing way up there so high, honey?" she called softly.

Sabrina hadn't answered, not wanting to get in trouble with her father or, worse, get him in trouble. Her father had made it a habit of sneaking out most nights to the Drunken Dory, a bar down the street, after he thought she had fallen asleep. Once he left, Sabrina would take a flashlight from under her pillow and slip out onto roof outside the bathroom window to watch the clouds and stars and to forget how scary it was to be alone at night.

Ruth, who owned the diner next door and six tiny motel cottages behind it, knew who Sabrina was. Once in a while, when he felt guilty and had a little money, her father would take her to the diner for macaroni and cheese or grilled cheese and tomato soup.

"Sabrina, honey, say this with me: 'I, Sabrina, am not afraid. I, Sabrina, am fearless. I, Sabrina, am not afraid. I, Sabrina, am fearless.'"

Ruth kept repeating those words until Sabrina joined her. "I, Sabrina, am not afraid. I, Sabrina, am fearless." Sabrina's voice grew louder with Ruth's and she began to say the word "fearless" with vigor. Ruth continued chanting the refrain with Sabrina as she slid out a ladder she kept leaning against the diner to the side of the house. She wiped her hands on her apron and started climbing up the rungs, all the while joining in: "I, Sabrina, am not afraid. I, Sabrina, am fearless."

When she reached Sabrina, Ruth opened her arms. Sabrina leaned forward, trusting that Ruth would lead her to safety, feeling Ruth's heart pounding against her as she smelled the stale cigarette smoke on Ruth's apron.

Once safely on the ground, Ruth let Sabrina down and took her hand.

"I think a brave little girl like you has earned herself some ice cream, don't you?" Sabrina had nodded and followed her through the kitchen of the diner, which was closed, into the dining area, where Ruth placed her on a stool with a shiny red vinyl cover.

"Vanilla or chocolate? Or maybe strawberry?"

She chose strawberry and dug into the huge mound of ice cream Ruth placed on the counter in front of her.

Ruth picked up the receiver to the turquoise phone on the wall and dialed a number, speaking softly so Sabrina couldn't hear her words. She wasn't worried about who she was calling. She knew she was safe with Ruth. No harm would come to her now.

Sabrina had been right about Ruth. When her father had staggered into the diner twenty minutes later, Ruth marched him through the swinging doors into the kitchen and lambasted him. Sabrina never knew what Ruth said, but from that day until the day Sabrina left for college, she and her father lived in one of Ruth's little motel cottages behind the diner.

"I, Sabrina, am not afraid. I, Sabrina, am fearless." Sabrina had said those words so many times that she thought they were probably carved inside her forehead— before she took the entrance exam for the pricy private high school her maternal grandmother had paid for in an effort to assuage her guilt for her mother's abandonment of Sabrina, before she went out on her first date with a boy who had to pick her up at the diner so Ruth could check him out, before she interviewed after college for a position at WXYZ as weekend meteorologist, before going on air and trying to sound like she was as normal as any young woman who'd grown up on Main Street, USA, and before she went on trial for first-degree murder of her husband.

Kelly's life may have been more privileged than Sabrina's, but Sabrina suspected it had as many fears and demons in it.

"Stay with me tonight. I'll call Mara and explain," Sabrina was surprised to hear herself say.

Kelly, Seth, and Neil all looked at her as if she'd just landed from another planet.

"Really?" Kelly asked.

"Really."

"Seth and I will take off and let you girls chat away," said Neil. "Just as soon as Seth tells us a little about what happened at the police station earlier." Sabrina was grateful Neil still had her back.

"Oh, you mean when they asked me to come in and give a statement?" Seth asked. His naiveté was both endearing and annoying.

"Yes. What did they ask and what did you tell them?" Neil asked, sounding like a lawyer again.

"Did you clean the pool at Villa Mascarpone that morning?" Sabrina asked, wanting the answer to that question first.

"I get to ask the questions, Salty, although that's a good one," Neil said. "Start with that one. Did you clean the pool?"

"Sure, first thing. Right before I did the Banks', like always," Seth said. Sabrina realized Seth worked much as Henry and she did. They had their own schedules and got their business done with little or no interaction with others.

Kelly sat back on the rocker, beginning to gently rock back and forth, appearing more relaxed when the conversation turned to murder than when it was focused on her father.

"Was Carter Johnson there? Did you see him?" Sabrina asked over Neil's frown. She was desperate to understand what had happened for her own sanity and to get everyone else off her back.

"Yeah, he was inside and said hello when I called out, saying I was there to clean the pool," Seth said. For the first time, he reached for the Sam Adams beer sitting next to his chair and took a chug.

"Did he say anything to you?" Neil asked.

"Just something like he'd taken his last dip and to go to it."

"Could you see what he was doing inside? Did you ever go into the house?" Neil asked.

"No, I never go into houses. Not a good idea. I learned early when one of the female houseguests asked me to come in and help her turn on the dishwasher and decided what she wanted to do was turn me on instead," Seth said, a mischievous smile across his face.

"We decided that it was best to have a policy that the pool person was prohibited from entering any of our villas after that, Neil. Too much exposure for Ten Villas, and Seth felt pretty uncomfortable," Sabrina added. The truth was Henry and Sabrina were never sure about what had happened on that occasion. Seth was a devilishly delicious-looking young man, always arriving to clean the pools barefoot and in his bathing suit, which made sense, given his line of work. But he was young and they knew very little about him, other than he showed up on time and did his job.

"So what did you tell the cops?" Neil asked.

"Just what I told you. That I saw Carter Johnson from the pool. He had stuff on the dining room table. It looked like he was packing, but I couldn't see what from the distance through the screens. I cleaned the pool and left. He was still there."

"What else did Janquar ask you?" Neil asked.

"He wanted to know if I had seen anyone else. He asked if anyone from Ten Villas had been there."

Anyone from Ten Villas? Sabrina knew that meant her. Janquar wanted Seth to implicate her and it infuriated her.

"What did you say?" Neil asked. Sabrina thought she saw Neil holding his breath.

"I said I was the only person at Villa Mascarpone. The people at Ten Villas wouldn't come until the guest had checked out," Seth said.

"Okay, what about anyone else? Did you see anyone in the area, even on the ride out or back?" Neil asked.

"The only other person I saw that morning was Mr. Banks pulling into his driveway just as I was leaving," Seth said.

Chapter Twenty-Nine

"Why are you calling me?" Henry asked, his heart pounding in his ears. He hadn't heard David's voice since the day his lawyer had told him he had to stop all communications with him, including the midnight drunk dialing they'd both engaged in, or he would lose not only his job but also the settlement that would let him start over.

"How could I not? I just saw on INN that there's been a murder on St. John at one of the villas you manage. Of course I called," David said, the concern in his voice sounding genuine to Henry. But how could he ever trust any word he spoke? David had betrayed him, and during those late-night calls, Henry always let him know how contemptuous he found his behavior.

"I don't know. I'm still trying to figure out how you could put the screws to me with your wife and with my job, David. I don't know how you do anything. I don't know how you put your head on your pillow at night and sleep, with all you did."

"I know, I know. I was a beast. A Judas, like you said. I don't suppose it matters how much I'm paying for it, does it? You probably don't want to hear what's gone on here, how I am an outcast at work—"

"No, I don't," Henry said, meaning it. He was surprised he didn't want to savor the details about how miserable David was, how karma had got its man. Henry had put David behind him. He hadn't forgotten him, hadn't really stopped loving him. No, what he had done was finally accept that his life would not be as he had planned, and that had liberated him. He no longer missed the airline staff he had considered part of his family. He had a new family of friends on a small island and a business he was proud to call his. It was bad enough that his new life was being threatened by Carter Johnson's murder, but did David think he could be yanked back into the past just because he was vulnerable? Could he?

"When I heard about the murder, Henry, and that it was at one of the villas you and that woman manage, I had to call and make sure you were okay. I saw Faith Chase beginning another crusade of destruction against your partner. I'm worried about you, Henry. I don't want to see you swept into the brutal media frenzy Sabrina attracts. That's why I called. That, and because I still love you. I always will," David said. Henry thought he might be crying.

"I'd be better off if you hated me, given how you show your love," Henry said.

"Do you really hate me, Henry?" Henry could hear the misery in David's voice, the pain he had heard night after night on those secret telephone calls, when David would try to explain why he had screwed Henry over; how much David needed his pilot's license, even if the airlines booted him; and how his wife could ruin him at work and destroy him financially.

"Are you still with her?" Henry asked, not wanting to but needing to know. David's silence was his answer.

Henry pushed the *off* button on the phone.

Chapter Thirty

After Neil and Seth left, Sabrina punched in the numbers to Mara's home phone, picturing Mara frantic with worry about Kelly's whereabouts. She hoped Rory wasn't home to add to Mara's troubles. She'd watched Rory Eagan at Bar None. He could be very charming and engaging with tourists, particularly with young beautiful female ones. He was bright enough and sometimes even funny. And he was very good looking—until you got to know him, and then his good looks faded.

Rory had hit on Sabrina when she'd first arrived on St. John. She had been drinking pretty regularly to numb the wounds still raw from the trial and had apparently lacerated his ego publicly at Bar None. Rory had been hostile to her ever since.

When he answered on the third ring, Sabrina could tell he was drunk.

"What do you want?" Rory asked when Sabrina asked for Mara.

"I want to speak to Mara. Please," Sabrina said, hating to take any guff from him but knowing Mara needed and deserved to know where Kelly was.

"We don't want you calling here. You've disgraced the whole island on national television. That woman, what's her name? Making St. John sound like a crime mecca. Why don't you just pack up and leave St. John to those of us who deserve to live here?" Rory said, cutting off the telephone call.

Sabrina sat still, stunned. At the moment, her priority was to let Mara know Kelly was with her and safe. But when the dust settled and Carter Johnson's murderer was in custody, Sabrina planned to have a conversation with Rory Eagan to let him know that he was the one who didn't deserve to live here. She decided to try to call Mara on her cell phone, hoping this would be part of the 50 percent of the time when there was cell phone reception out there at the end of Fish Bay. When Mara picked up, Sabrina could hear the concern in her voice.

"I was just about to get in the car and go look for her," Mara said after Sabrina told her Kelly was with her and that Seth had brought Kelly there, thinking it was a safe place.

"She's fine, Mara, although pretty upset about the confrontation with Rory and Seth."

"It was awful. I'm sure she's embarrassed that Rory behaved like that in public," Mara said, and Sabrina could hear that she got it. Sabrina wondered what a public humiliation would do to a sensitive, even fragile adolescent.

They agreed Kelly would stay with Sabrina and that Mara would pick her up in the morning to catch the ferry to St. Thomas and get her back into her routine before she thought twice about it.

"Okay," Sabrina said to Kelly, who was still rocking on her chair but now with Sabrina's permission. "All set with Mara."

"Is she mad at me?"

"She didn't sound it," Sabrina said, not really wanting to become involved in parental politics.

"I feel bad for her," Kelly said.

"How so?" Sabrina asked, figuring Kelly wanted to tell her. She was always hearing confessions, revelations, and secret information for some reason. At the television station, she'd known who was sleeping with whom, who'd had "work" done, and when someone was negotiating a new contract with another station. She'd kept her mouth shut about it all because she didn't want to get involved with the messes people created in their own lives. That had only seemed to encourage people to tell her more. Sabrina figured she could at least lend an ear to a kid who had the misfortune to be the daughter of Rory Eagan.

"My father isn't very nice to her, even though she's a great stepmother to me and Liam. She's taken care of us since we were four," Kelly said, pulling her knees in and placing her feet under her. She smiled for the first time that evening, and Sabrina thought her grin looked mischievous and slightly familiar.

"How old are you anyway?" Sabrina asked, thinking she seemed more worldly than most teenagers, which surprised her, given that she was raised on an island.

"Seventeen. One more year here on this miserable island and then I get to go to college. I might go to Boston or New York," Kelly said, clearly excited. "Except, I don't know now that I've met Seth. I don't think I can leave him. Maybe he'll have to leave St. John too."

Oh dear God, Sabrina thought. Does it start this early? A beautiful young woman, clearly bright and articulate, with a stepmother willing to write a check to any of the best colleges, and Kelly might sacrifice it all for a boyfriend? She wondered if they were sleeping together. She hoped they weren't, knowing that they probably were.

"Keep your options open," Sabrina said, not wanting to anger her.

"I just wish Liam were home so Mara wouldn't have to be alone with him. Or that those people weren't at Villa Mascarpone so that he could leave and go to his other house," Kelly said, now frowning. She was as beautiful frowning as she was smiling.

"His other house?" Sabrina asked.

"That's what we call it. When he gets ugly or comes home totaled after closing Bar None, he stays next door."

Next door? With the Banks? Were they that kind to their neighbors? The only other house was Villa Mascarpone.

Sabrina had to know. "With the Banks?" she asked. "They are very nice folks, aren't they?"

"The old people? Yeah, I guess they're nice. I don't really know, except Mrs. Banks sends over some great desserts sometimes. No, at the rental villa. Mara has extra keys," Kelly said and then seemed to realize this was something she should not be telling her. Sabrina said nothing and tried to stay expressionless.

"She always goes over and cleans up after him. I've even helped her," Kelly said. "Please don't tell Mara I told you. I'm already screwed. It's just, we need to get him out of the house before . . ."

Before what? Sabrina thought. Before he hit one of them? Before he got so ugly and belligerent his words were worse than blows?

"Don't worry, honey," Sabrina said, meaning it but not promising her she wouldn't have a conversation with Mara. She would, but Kelly would never know about it.

Chapter Thirty-One

Deirdre flung open the gate to the pool and stepped inside the courtyard, her heart in her throat. She could see Sam through the glass sliding doors. He was putting the bar stools back in their proper place, and she knew he had probably wiped the feet of each clean of any dirt from the path. He was always cleaning up after her, tidying up her messes, and tonight it broke her heart to know she didn't deserve this kind man.

He came to her as soon as she slipped through the doors but said nothing.

"I've lost them, Sam," Deirdre said, her voice flat.

"What happened, honey?" he asked.

"Nothing. Everything. I met Kelly. I saw Kelly. She's not my daughter."

"You can't be saying . . . He was so sure. I know she's older, but we expected some surprises," Sam said, taking Deirdre by the hand and walking her over to sit on the sofa. A single nectarine-colored hibiscus Sam had picked for her earlier sat on the glass coffee table floating in a martini glass.

"I don't mean that. I mean it's too late. She's already a beautiful young woman, spirited, independent. She's already who she is. There is no room or time for me to be part of any of that," Deirdre said.

She looked over at Sam, who had remained quiet. He always seemed to know when to speak and when to be silent. He had tears in his eyes, and she knew they were for her.

"The stepmother seems to be a very good person. Kind, but firm, with a sense of humor. I should be grateful that she's done such a good job. I am grateful for that. But it's her influence, her ideas, her values that have shaped Liam and Kelly into the people they are today, the people they will always be. They don't know me. They have nothing that comes from me, Sam."

"I don't think that's entirely true. You cannot discount how important those first four years were. They were the formative ones, you know. How many experts have we talked to? Books have we read? They all say the same thing. A mother's early influence when attachment is forming is irreplaceable. Please give yourself credit for that much."

"But do I disrupt their lives now? There is very little I can offer them, other than proof that their father is a horrid man, which I believe they already know. Certainly, Kelly does. She was pretty vocal about it tonight," Deirdre said.

Sam reached over and took her two hands in his.

"You listen to me, Deirdre Leonard. Your children deserve to know the truth. They deserve to know they have a mother who loves them, who has always loved them and never stopped looking for them. What they do with it is up to them. They have the right to know that he's been lying to them: that you are not dead, were never an alcoholic who slammed into a tree, and that they were taken from you. We now know he has told that to anyone who will listen since he came to St. John. Certainly, your children must have heard the lie. He took those children from you, but he also took you from those children. He is the one who needs to be held accountable. If not by you, then by his own children," Sam said, his voice growing more passionate as he gripped her hands in his.

"So after all of the years, all of the anguish, are you saying you are ready to walk away from your children after finally finding them? Are you afraid about how they will receive you, now that you finally saw Kelly?" Sam let Deirdre's hands fall away.

"Maybe. But no, of course I can't walk away. I'm just realizing how I can't undo what has happened. It's a wrong that can never be righted."

"What do you want to do? You know I will support any decision you make."

"I just don't know what to do, how to approach the situation. Our plans relied on him connecting us with the authorities. I can't just knock on the door with the big reveal. And we can't assume that Joel's death isn't somehow connected to his investigation. Shouldn't we let the police know why he was here, what he was doing?"

Deirdre felt like her head might explode with all the complications that surrounded her. Was Joel's murder connected to what he'd been investigating? Would her children believe that she had always loved them and that she wasn't showing up at the eleventh hour of their adolescence just to make it more painful? Could she ever have a sliver of their hearts, or had Mara filled all the space intended for her?

"I've been thinking the same thing. I wouldn't ever do anything to interfere with your reunion with your children, but I do think we owe some kind of obligation to the man who found them for you. I just don't want to go directly to the police. I've wondered if we couldn't consult Neil Perry first. He's got the kind of mind that can absorb the sensitive considerations we have on our hands."

Sam stood and went over to Deirdre, putting his arms around her.

"You're right, Sam. He'd at least offer us some objectivity. I can't think straight anymore and I know I must be making it difficult for you. I'm sorry to bring all of this into your world, I really am," Deirdre said, stepping into Sam's embrace.

"It's *our* world, honey, *our* world. Don't ever apologize for our life."

Chapter Thirty-Two

Over a cup of French roast coffee, Henry set three goals for the day. First, he would call Elaine Kimball back and figure out what she had been babbling about on the telephone. Next, he would get back the laptops from Detective Janquar. Last, and most important, he would not think about David's telephone call last night. Not for one fleeting second.

He'd been awakened early by the randy rooster who lived down the hill from him. No need for an alarm clock in his neighborhood or throughout most of St. John. Henry made it a practice to warn guests that roosters, pigs, goats, donkeys, deer, and mongoose roamed freely throughout St. John. That was part of its charm.

Henry decided he wouldn't call Sabrina until he had something coherent to say about the Elaine Kimball situation. It had gotten so crazy over the past several days that he wasn't sure if he'd even mentioned the weird telephone conversation he'd had with Elaine. Henry had gotten very good at knowing which customers and owners were inclined to call when they were a little tipsy, but Elaine wasn't one of them. He waited until 8:00 a.m. on the dot and made the call.

"Hi Elaine, Henry Whitman from Ten Villas calling again. Have you settled in after your trip?"

"We have, Henry. And as gorgeous as Hawaii was, I don't know if I can wait for a whole year to come back to St. John. I wish we'd won the lottery instead of this contest so I could buy a villa on St. John. Not that we're not grateful, of course. We are, Henry. I hope you told Sabrina," Elaine said, sounding buzzed with caffeine, which he hoped would bring clarity to her tale about the contest.

"Elaine, sweetie, let me be frank. Things here on the island have been a little crazy. I told you about the man who died at Villa Mascarpone. And it seems some funny stuff has been going on. Like that contest. Can you tell me a little more about it? Like who contacted you?"

"Clinton Taylor? Well, I only talked to the man twice. The first time I really didn't believe what he had to say. But when he sent the tickets and itinerary, I thought maybe this is legit. John said I should call you or Sabrina, but when I mentioned it to Clinton, he said he'd been hired by you guys to run the contest, that it's what he does for a living. He said these kinds of contests, where someone gets the dream trip of a lifetime, pay for themselves, that people like you use them for advertising. And that all we had to do was allow our names and photos to be used in some ads for Ten Villas in which we say, 'I'd rather be in St. John.' Which is true, of course."

"I see," said Henry, but he didn't. "Did this guy tell you the value of the vacation?"

"Not exactly, but he mentioned that the villas were five grand a week and we flew first class, so you can kind of figure it out. Why are you asking me this stuff, Henry? It was your contest. Didn't your business have to pay for all of this and for Mr. Taylor?"

"Actually, Elaine, we didn't. That's the problem. I don't know anyone named Clinton Taylor, and while Sabrina and I are pleased with how Ten Villas is doing, we're not in a position to be giving away twenty-five-thousand-dollar vacations, even for advertising purposes." Henry said, figuring there really was no reason not to just tell her the truth, which was becoming a rare commodity on St. John. Then he remembered something Elaine had said earlier.

"How did you know that Villa Mascarpone would be rented for the month when you normally are there?" he asked.

"Mr. Taylor told me. Henry, this is sounding very creepy to me. Do you think I should do something?"

"Give me 'til tomorrow to see if I can figure this out, Elaine. I know you're trying to do what's right, but there are enough fingers down here wagging in different directions to make quite a commotion. Let's not get you in the thick of it, if it can be avoided," Henry said, genuinely feeling bad that Elaine was being drawn into a mess.

"Thanks, Henry. You'll keep me posted?"

"That I will," Henry said, signing off, wondering why someone would pay twenty-five grand to send the Kimballs to Hawaii and give Ten Villas the credit for doing it. And why did these names sound like they belonged on Mount Rushmore? Clinton Taylor. Carter Johnson. All mixed and matched names of former presidents. He was pretty sure Carter Johnson and Clinton Taylor were the same guy and no president.

Chapter Thirty-Three

The next morning, Sabrina found Kelly sprawled all over the sofa, sheets draping over her as though she were a Greek goddess with honey red hair. Sabrina wondered if she was ever that beautiful. And if she had been, had anyone appreciated it? She certainly hadn't. Why do women never know their own beauty until it is lost and only left to regret?

They'd had a nice chat about St. John, college, and New England and had stayed clear of the topic of men. Sabrina wasn't in a hurry to learn more about Kelly's relationship with Seth and she definitely didn't want to field questions about the one she didn't have with Neil.

Sabrina brewed coffee and got into her shower, even though it was raining and the shower had no roof.

She offered Kelly use of the shower, but Kelly declined, saying she had just showered before she went out the evening before.

Mara arrived with Kelly's clean school uniform—which all students in the Virgin Islands wore, whether in private or public school—just as Neil called to tell Sabrina there were some new developments in the case that he couldn't discuss on the telephone. She told him she'd hop a ride with Mara, who was bringing Kelly to the ferry.

"How was the slumber party, Salty? I bet you and Kelly had a pretty nice time," Neil said.

"Actually, we did. Remind me to tell you something," she said, not wanting to forget to let Neil know that Rory Eagan had a key to Villa Mascarpone. Sabrina wondered if the police knew, but she doubted it. She knew the murder had taken place outside of the house, but still, having access to a home where a murder occurred had to count for something, didn't it?

Or did it? So far, Sabrina knew so many bits and pieces, which individually meant nothing. But, she wondered, could those chips create a mosaic picture that made sense of all the parts?

The difference in Kelly's appearance on the porch the evening before and this morning in the backseat of Mara's car was remarkable. Today she looked like the schoolgirl she was. The night before, she'd looked like a young woman in love. Sabrina was glad, not for the first time in her life, that motherhood had passed her by. She didn't think she was equipped for the job.

Kelly thanked Sabrina for her hospitality before she got out of the car and onto the ferry, a matter Mara did not let go to chance, watching her board and remaining at the dock until the ferry sailed. They drove over to the back of Bar None and chatted before Sabrina went to find Neil.

"Funny, I never get to come to this place," Mara said. "I guess it might get a little crowded if I did." She gave Sabrina a knowing smile. Sabrina grinned back. What else was she to do?

"At least you don't have to have a container blockading your home from the rest of the world," Sabrina said, wanting to commiserate with her.

"No, but if you need me to build you a fortress, just give me a jingle. It's what I do best."

They laughed an easy laugh between two women whose lives just didn't seem to stay on track.

"Thanks for inviting Kelly to stay last night. It was better she wasn't home. After Rory and Seth nearly came to blows, I don't think Kelly could have handled much more. Especially when Lee came to interview us. Talk about a dark and stormy night."

"Who's Lee?"

"Janquar. Leon Janquar. The police detective. He wanted to interview everyone who lived up on the hill to see if we remembered seeing anything or anybody. Rory had been avoiding it. I've known Lee for years. He's a big teddy bear under all that serious police business."

Teddy Bear? Janquar? In the same sentence? That didn't work for Sabrina. But she kept her opinion of the detective to herself, wanting to learn more.

"How did it go?"

"Oh, Rory had a few drinks in him, so he got belligerent and tested Lee's patience. Neither of us have alibis for that morning. I mean, I was around Cruz Bay doing errands and at some building sites, but not in one spot the entire time. And Rory, well, he sleeps pretty late and then he goes on the computer, so he can't really back up where he was. Not that we're suspects, but I guess it's helpful if the police can pin down where people were and what they remembered seeing," Mara said, turning the air conditioner up.

"Did either of you see anything? They are all over me because I found the body," Sabrina said, not pulling any punches. She needed help and knew it.

"I didn't. Rory only saw you and the Bankses after the police got there when he was leaving to come here—to town, I mean. He mentioned seeing you at Villa Mascarpone one afternoon but couldn't put a date on it. It was probably the afternoon the guy arrived," Mara said, then added, "Oh, I almost forgot. Did the people in Villa Mascarpone get in touch with you or Henry? The woman with the strawberry blonde hair came over last night, right in the middle of Kelly's snit, to see if we were having power surges. I told her we weren't. What's with them wanting to stay in a house where someone's just been murdered, anyway?"

Yes, what was with that? Sabrina decided that she needed to get a grasp on the Leonards, especially since they had at least spoken to Carter Johnson on the telephone while he was a guest. But here was her opening about the key.

"You know, Mara, I appreciate you being the contact guests in Villa Mascarpone can reach out to if there's a problem, but I can understand it if it's gotten a bit much," she said.

"No, no, Sabrina, it's nothing. It's what we do here on an island, help each other. You know that. Look what you did for Kelly last night. And I've always had a key to Villa Mascarpone, even before you and Henry managed it. I used to have one to the Banks's house before they bought it, when it was a rental. I probably still do," Mara said, her words slowing as she spoke them. She looked directly at Sabrina.

"You know, don't you?" Mara asked. "You know about Rory's 'other house.'"

"Yes, but you mustn't blame Kelly."

"Kelly? She's the last person I'd blame. I blame me. I'm the one responsible here. I shouldn't have let it go on, but . . ." Mara's voice trailed off.

"It gets pretty bad, I guess," Sabrina said.

"You know, if I can give Rory credit for anything, it's for how he knew to get the kids away from Massachusetts after their mother killed herself, to let them start fresh in what he saw as a perfect place to raise kids. But he's never given up the anger he had for Dee, and she's been dead how many years? He drinks, gets mean, and it's just too much. I tell him he has to leave until he sobers up. At some point, he found the keys to Villa Mascarpone and decided it would be his home away from home when there were no guests there. I figured it out right away when he would show up the next day on foot, his car still in the garage. But I let it go."

"I see," Sabrina said, because she did. She'd seen enough of Rory Eagan to understand why Mara's relief could let her ignore what he was doing.

"I'm sorry, really, I am. I know it was deceptive. I always went over and cleaned up after him when he stayed there, but I know that doesn't make it right. I just needed to get him away from the kids, especially Kelly. Once she began looking like a young woman, Rory started to get angry with her, more than just annoyed. I got scared."

"Do the police know about the key, Mara?"

"No, I didn't tell them. Lee was asking a lot of questions about Evan Banks. I got the impression that he was concerned Evan's dementia, or whatever he has, might have caught up with him."

"I think Janquar has to know, Mara," Sabrina said firmly, refusing to address him as either Detective or Lee. He wasn't her buddy and she wasn't so sure how great a detective he was if he hadn't found out who else had a key to Villa Mascarpone.

"You're right. I'll go see Lee personally and let him know. Why don't you come with me, Sabrina? I know you and Lee haven't been on good terms ever since you had a villa broken into, and now this murder at Villa Mascarpone doesn't seem to be helping. Look, I'll be honest, Sabrina. I know the cops resented you coming to live here after you were acquitted. I think some of them think you got away with, well, murder," Mara said. "Come with me when I talk to Janquar and I can show him you are my friend."

Sabrina liked the sound of that much better than the getting away with murder part. She appreciated Mara's offer to demonstrate to Janquar that she was one of them now.

"I can't go until later this afternoon. I have to meet with Neil and Henry in a few minutes and then Henry and I have three houses to prepare for guests," Sabrina said.

"That works for me. I'm heading over to the East End to meet with some people who want to build a house. A six-thousand-square-foot house. That would keep me busy and pay for some college tuition, now, wouldn't it?" Mara said.

The two women agreed to meet mid-afternoon.

As Sabrina got out of the jeep, Mara asked, "How can a man alone on a vacation on an island generally considered safe get murdered and screw up the lives of strangers?"

Chapter Thirty-Four

Sabrina slipped under the straw curtain door to Neil's office, feeling more relaxed after her conversation with Mara. She was ready to tackle the three villas that needed cleaning right after the meeting. It would feel good to be busy.

"Hey, Salty. You're looking no worse for the wear this morning," Neil said, clearing his throat. "Sit down and listen to this."

Neil sat opposite Henry, a thermal carafe of coffee sitting between them. Sabrina slid next to Henry, who sipped a glass of tomato juice with a slice of lemon while he spilled the story about Elaine Kimball.

"So you're telling me someone paid about twenty-five grand for a vacation in Hawaii and gave Ten Villas credit for it? Why would someone do that? Do you guys have that kind of money? Have you got a fairy godmother?"

Henry shrugged his shoulders.

"I have no benefactors. I had to cash in my retirement from the airline and combine it with the settlement

I got to buy my condo and my share of the business with Sabrina. I have a little nest egg left, but not the kind of money to finance some crazy advertising scheme," Henry said, sounding more serious.

"The same goes for me. Hey, whatever happened to the INN crew? Are they still stuck at Gibney?" Sabrina asked, helping herself to a mug of coffee and offering to refill Neil's, as if this were her tea party.

Neil started to laugh, Henry joining him.

"What? Let me in on the joke. I could use a laugh," Sabrina said.

"Well, those reporters finally did reach Fred Sinkhole here at the bar, just as we were closing. Fred decided they were trespassing, that they had interfered with use of public property on the island, so he called up someone in the Department of Public Works and made them go and tow the news van. It's impounded at DPW until INN pays a big fat fine and the paperwork to release it is processed. You do know how long that takes on an island, don't you, Salty?" Neil asked, arching his eyebrows.

"But Neil heard they've rented a jeep, so you still have to have your eyes wide open."

"What did you want to tell me that you couldn't over the telephone?" Sabrina asked Neil.

"I stopped by the police station this morning to get the items taken from your house. It was mostly lists of your guests and which houses they stay in. Henry was already there, retrieving your laptops. They showed up at his condo with a search warrant right after I took you and Girlfriend for your swim. Found diddlysquat, but whatever. They did what cops do. Look at the most logical suspects. But now they know who Carter Johnson was and where he lived, so the possibilities are wide open," Neil said with a small smile at the corners of his mouth. Sabrina could see Neil enjoyed delivering a little good news, even in small doses. "His real name is Joel Levin. He owns a private investigation firm in New York City called Presidential Investigations Inc. He's a one-man shop, but according to Janquar, he's highly respected and discreet. He specializes in finding people who have disappeared. He lived in New Jersey. No wife, but two exes. Let's keep this to ourselves 'til Janquar goes public with this information," Neil said.

"Well, I guess that proves my gaydar is way off," Henry said, shrinking down a little in the bench.

"How did they find this out?" Sabrina asked.

"Fingerprints. To get a PI license, you have to be fingerprinted. Levin's prints came up when they were run through the national registry. Now Lee's got to work through the police in New York and New Jersey to come up with more background on Levin to see if there's anything to suggest who might want to kill him," Neil said.

"I thought he was a photographer. All of those pictures sitting on the dining room table," Henry said.

"Investigators take photos. Just like journalists. So was he here on an assignment or was he on a vacation?"

Sabrina asked, taking note that now Neil was referring to Janquar as Lee, which was a little unsettling.

"We don't know. Neither do the police," Neil said.

"You have to wonder," said Henry. "What next?"

"How about the fact that Mara and Rory have been using the spare key to access Villa Mascarpone?" Sabrina said. Henry looked at Neil, who was shaking his head.

"And I thought I'd moved to paradise and left all of my worries behind," Neil said.

Chapter Thirty-Five

Henry and Sabrina left Bar None with no time to talk about the mind-boggling new developments in the case. They had three houses emptying, two of which had new occupants arriving on the afternoon ferry. Sabrina had no idea where Tanya was, so enlisting her help wasn't an option. It was just the two of them once again.

Henry drove them in his neighbor's car to the Ten Villas van he had parked up by the cemetery. They got into the van and were off to Casa Bougainvillea, a smaller home in nearby Chocolate Hole.

It was a charming two-bedroom home, one of only two they had without pools. The Falveys, the couple who had stayed there, were repeat guests. Henry and Sabrina hoped the house would be clean, and they were right.

The Falveys had left the house spotless. The refrigerator wiped clean, beds stripped, laundry ready to go in the washer room, floors vacuumed, dishwasher empty. In the freezer was half a bottle of vodka, which Sabrina immediately put in her cleaning bag while Henry grabbed the chocolates left in the fridge.

Sabrina took one bathroom and Henry the other. Even though the rooms didn't need to be done, they at least needed to say they had done something. After the bathrooms were done, they took clean linens and went to the bedrooms to make the beds.

Henry had been uncharacteristically quiet, but Sabrina said nothing, thinking he needed time to absorb all the details that were emerging regarding the case. He broke his silence as they turned the king-size sheets in different directions to find where the top was.

"David called me last night," he said, as if he were telling her to turn the bottom sheet one more time.

Sabrina stopped and dropped her corner.

"No," she said.

"He did," Henry said, finally looking at her.

"Why? What did he say?"

"That he'd seen what was happening here. That he was worried about me. That he loves me."

"What did you do?" she asked, not being able to read Henry's blank expression.

"I hung up on him,"

"And?"

"And nothing," Henry said. "I'm just sharing."

"Are you okay?" Sabrina asked as they lifted the top sheet above the bed and let it float down to the mattress like a kite landing.

"Yes. No. I don't know," Henry said.

"Do you want to talk about it?"

"Not yet. I need to process it," Henry said. "Process" was one of the words Henry used when he tried explaining to her why she would benefit from having a therapist. Sabrina couldn't justify paying a stranger to listen to her troubles when she had a friend who would do it for free.

"How was the swim with Neil?"

Sabrina knew he wanted to know more than how warm the water was.

"Fine," she said.

They pulled the coverlet up and began putting pillows into their cases after Henry sprayed lavender mist on them.

"Henry," she said, not knowing how to begin the conversation she knew would turn into a confession.

He looked over at her and said nothing, but Sabrina knew he was waiting for more.

"Something happened at Villa Mascarpone that I need to talk about," she said.

"Jesus, you didn't kill whatever-his-name-is, did you?" Henry had turned pale on her.

"No, I had sex with him," she said.

"That's all? Thank God." Henry sprayed the lavender mist into the air.

"You don't think that's a big deal?" she asked.

Henry flopped down onto the bed they had just finished making. She collapsed next to him.

"Do you?"

"Well, if he hadn't gotten murdered, probably not," Sabrina said.

"Tell me about it. I mean, how you ended up having sex with him. You know, whose idea it was. Not exactly what happened, unless you feel the need to reveal the actual details. Then I'll listen," Henry said and she had to laugh.

"He had run out of propane. When I brought out the replacement tank, he stood out on the back deck while I hooked it up."

Henry only needed the *Reader's Digest* version of the story, not the details about a connection.

"We chatted a little. I found him attractive. He must have found me passable. He was alone on an island. I hadn't been with a man since . . ." Her throat caught. It was true. She hadn't had sex since Ben.

"Well, that sounds natural enough. And sweetie, you are more than passable."

"Do you think I need to tell the police about the propane? About the sex?" Sabrina asked, feeling better just having put the question out there rather than having the weight of it sitting on her chest, suffocating her.

"No, Sabrina. Having sex with a man who happened to die a couple of days later has nothing to do with his murder. There is no reason to tell the police and there is no reason Neil ever has to know. You're worried about that, too, aren't you?"

"Uh-huh," she said, admitting it to herself for the first time. She liked Neil Perry. He was good looking, fun, and she was beginning to trust him, something Sabrina had thought she would never say about a man again.

Henry leaped up off the bed. "Great. You are alive and well, and maybe a little sex with a stranger was just the jump-start you needed."

"And what about you, Henry?"

"We'll just have to wait and see about that one, honey."

Chapter Thirty-Six

Sabrina tackled the third house on her own, sending Henry to meet and greet guests at the dock. That she preferred toilet bowls to people said something about her, she knew, but she enjoyed the quiet up on Mamey Peak where Last Call was located. Guests wouldn't be arriving until the next day, so she had taken her time, even enjoying a glass of ice water on the deck before she gathered her supplies to leave.

She thought she heard something outside, but the sliders were closed because it was drizzling. She figured it was a roaming goat or donkey, because she didn't hear an engine. Henry had called to say the guests had all arrived and had been delivered to their respective villas. Maybe life was getting back to normal.

Henry also had told her he was picking up Liam and Kelly for Mara because she had a midafternoon appointment. Sabrina hoped she hadn't complicated Mara's life too much by insisting she tell Janquar about the keys, but it was important information and maybe even a test of their budding friendship.

The rain had finally stopped, but the deck was still slippery, so Sabrina was cautious when she stepped outside the house to pack up the car. She loved how routine and mundane the afternoon had felt. She wanted to celebrate, toast the beauty of an ordinary life. There might even be a good sunset tonight.

Sabrina walked by the pool and opened the gate to the driveway. Suddenly, she was blinded once again by lights she knew came from a high-powered television camera. Instinctively, she put her forearm across her eyes and stepped back toward the pool.

A figure silhouetted by the haze came toward her. A woman.

"Sabrina, Sabrina Salter. We have you live on camera and want to know, what do you think about being a person of interest in the death of Carter Johnson, a.k.a. Joel Levin? Are you worried you might be facing a murder trial for the second time in just a few years? Do you want to talk on camera and set the record straight about whether you have any involvement in the death of a guest at one of your villas?"

I, Sabrina, am not afraid. I, Sabrina, am fearless.

Ruth's words deafened the voice of the same reporter who had been on the beach the night before, when she and Girlfriend had emerged from their swim. Sabrina took a deep breath and smiled, stepping back once again toward the pool.

"Sure, I'll make a statement, if you promise to quote me accurately."

Now Sabrina could see the reporter and a cameraman behind her. They had probably arrived when she was vacuuming, which was why she hadn't heard them. Henry had warned her they would be all over the island looking for her. The Ten Villas website showed the location of all the villas. There was even a map with directions, for God's sake.

Sabrina put one foot forward and turned her body toward it, lifting her chin for the camera, just as she had learned to as a weather anchor. She felt ridiculous posing in flip-flops and shorts, but this would be an impromptu appearance. People love them.

The nameless reporter was decked out in silk pantsuit and sandals with heels. Her makeup seemed to be melting in the steamy humidity.

"Are you done primping for the camera?" the reporter asked, approaching Sabrina.

"Is it rolling?" Sabrina asked.

"Yes, it is. Now let's get down to business, Ms. Salter. Do you expect the American public to buy—"

Sabrina reached down, grabbed the cuff of one of the reporter's pant legs, tugged fast, making the woman lose her balance and fall backward into the pool. She made a large splash and began flailing and choking on water. Her assistant rushed to help her, diving in after her, because Sabrina realized the silly woman could not even swim.

Sabrina grabbed the opportunity to dump the camera and mikes in the pool.

Pulling a shoeless, drenched reporter from the pool, her associate, equally as wet but at least able to swim, told Sabrina she would pay for this.

"Oh, really? Pay for what?" Sabrina asked, pointing to the camera at the bottom of the pool. "For what happened when you trespassed?"

In five minutes, they were gone, and Sabrina locked up the house. She decided to call Neil and tell him what a good time she'd just had and to warn him that someone might be saying some vicious untruths about her.

She punched in his number. Sabrina was ready to put Neil on speed dial, a kind of commitment for her, when she heard his voice and knew something was awfully wrong.

"Hey Salty, I can't talk right now. I've got a situation. Can I catch you later?"

Chapter Thirty-Seven

Sabrina met Mara in the parking lot of the Elaine I. Sprauve Library. Henry had the van, so they drove in Henry's neighbor's borrowed vehicle directly to the police station a short distance away.

"I feel really bad I did this, Sabrina. This guilt reminds me of being in parochial school," Mara said.

Sabrina laughed.

Inside the police station, the desk sergeant ushered them into Janquar's office.

"Okay, Mara, what's on your mind? I'm kind of busy here," Janquar said, puffy circles under his eyes, his lids drooping, begging for sleep. He didn't ask her to sit, which Sabrina didn't take as a good sign. Then he seemed to notice she was standing next to Sabrina.

"Why are you here, Ms. Salter?" Janquar asked, sounding perplexed and annoyed. Very annoyed.

"I asked her to come, Lee."

"I can't talk to her without her lawyer," Janquar said.

"No, Detective Janquar. I don't need my lawyer for this."

"Look, Lee, I felt I should come and tell you something we didn't mention when you were at the house last night. I should have, but, well . . ."

Janquar rested his hands on his desk. "Mara, we've known each other a long time. What's on your mind?"

Mara plunged in, telling Janquar about the key and her husband's occasional use of Villa Mascarpone, stressing that neither Sabrina nor Henry had known about it until today. She told him how she would clean the villa afterward, so no one at Ten Villas would notice.

"I know it was wrong, Lee. Rory is difficult, but he is Liam's and Kelly's father, and I've tried to keep life on an even keel the best I can. I just thought you needed to know this," she said.

"I'll need to talk to Rory again. Do you know where he is?"

"Sure. He went out right after you left our house last night and wasn't home when I left this morning. I'm ninety-nine percent sure he's at home, in bed, sleeping it off."

"Follow me up there in case he doesn't hear me knocking, will you?" Janquar said, sighing.

"I'm driving her," Sabrina said, really asking for permission from Janquar.

"Sure, if it's okay with Mara," Janquar said.

"Lee, Sabrina is one of my closest friends on the island. Of course it's okay."

And they were off. During the ride, Mara talked about how life was about to change for all of them, even without a murder. The kids were looking at colleges online. In less than two years, they would be gone, off to build their own lives, make their own mistakes, which she hoped would be new ones, not a repetition of their father's and hers.

Sabrina looked in her rearview mirror as she began the final climb up the steep curve to the top of Fish Bay Road. Janquar's Envoy led the way.

Sabrina parked in one of the two spots outside Cairn Suantrai, leaving the other for Janquar. She wanted to be able to leave with Mara as quickly as possible after the interview.

She noticed the rental jeep over at Villa Mascarpone and hoped the Leonards had resolved their issues with the electricity. The Banks' jeep was gone. Sabrina hoped Lyla and Evan were busy volunteering.

Leon stepped out of the police van with as much grace as a man his size could. Sabrina offered to remain in the car, but Mara asked that she come with her.

"Frankly, this is making me more than a little nervous, Sabrina. I don't like confrontations, particularly with Rory," Mara said.

Sabrina watched Mara open the massive front door with a key after disengaging the security alarm with her password, "K-E-L-I." Everything in this woman's life was about her kids, Sabrina thought.

The unlikely threesome entered the huge front hall, which was dark, cool, and quiet. A tennis racket and a huge pair of sneakers sat against a wall with hooks for jackets, backpacks, and other accoutrements of adolescence.

"Rory," Mara called gently, walking into the kitchen. She felt the coffee pot and shook her head, signaling it hadn't been used recently.

"Maybe he's not home," Janquar said, after Mara called out three more times. She led them to a passageway to the right of the kitchen and opened a door to a garage where Rory's car was parked. Janquar leaned over and touched the hood.

"Cold. Maybe he's out for a walk."

Mara frowned.

"No, he must be still asleep in his room. We've had separate rooms for years. He stays in the guest room, down the hallway where the kids' rooms are. That's why I have to make him leave. It's just too close to the kids when he gets nasty after drinking."

They returned to the kitchen, entering the great hall again. Mara led Janquar down another passageway off the left of the hall. They passed a bedroom filled with ruffled pink-and-orange curtains and bedding, clothes piled high on a chair, a closet door open, and shoes spilled out onto the floor. Through a large window, there was a view of St. Thomas that people would pay millions for.

The next room was also open, more masculine but equally as cluttered and disorganized. Red Sox posters hung on walls, a soccer ball lay on the floor, and a guitar rested against the closed closet.

The door at the end of the corridor was closed.

Mara knocked gently at first.

"Rory? Rory, Lee Janquar is here to talk to us again," she said. When there was no response, Mara knocked harder, calling his name louder. Finally, she tugged on the doorknob, but it was locked.

"Here, let me have a try. Could he go out another way?" Janquar whispered.

"Not unless he wants to drop a hundred feet off the cliff," Mara said, stepping aside.

"Mr. Eagan, Detective Janquar here. Please open the door and come out. I have some follow-up questions for you, which won't take too long."

Still no response. Sabrina could see the muscles in Leon Janquar's face tighten.

"Sir, if you do not open this door immediately, I will have to assume you have experienced a medical emergency and that your health is in imminent danger. I will have to force the door open. I think you know I am capable of doing that."

Sabrina thought she heard voices before the sound of movement followed by the clatter of something falling on the tile floor. Was he still so drunk he was talking to himself?

Finally, the door swung fully open. Rory Eagan appeared wrapped in a sheet, like a Roman draped in a toga. Behind him, swathed in her own sheet, blonde hair tousled, face flushed with fear, sat a young woman in bed. A woman Sabrina recognized.

"Detective Janquar," Rory said, in exaggerated grandeur sweeping his right arm behind him toward the bed. "Please meet Tanya, the alibi I was reluctant to give you last night. Why is this woman in my home? Isn't she the prime suspect in a murder?" Rory pointed at Sabrina.

Sabrina didn't really care what Rory Eagan had to say about her. She was more outraged that he never even glanced at Mara, never cowered at being discovered in flagrante delicto or acknowledged the affront to his wife. But his disregard for her presence gave Mara the perfect opportunity to draw back the muscular arms that had built this home for his children and punch him with such force that he fell back onto the floor. Sabrina was duly impressed.

"Put some clothes on, Mr. Eagan, and do it fast," Janquar said.

"Detective, I have been assaulted. You saw her punch me. I insist you arrest her. We have a witness who saw this all," Rory said, still sitting on the floor. "Actually, we have two," he added, smiling at Sabrina.

"What I saw, Mr. Eagan, is a hung-over drunk trip and fall in his own sheets. I'm betting that's what Ms. Tanya saw too, if she saw anything. Two minutes. In your kitchen." Janquar took Mara by the elbow and led her out of the room and down the long corridor, Sabrina following behind.

Chapter Thirty-Eight

Deirdre hesitated before closing the periwinkle gate, even before noticing the police van was back at Kelly and Liam's house. They were off to town to talk to Neil Perry, who they'd called earlier that morning.

"Sam, do you think we ought to wait to make sure everything is okay with the kids before we go to Cruz Bay?" she asked, pulling her sun hat down lower on her head, not wanting to be exposed to the elements or inhabitants at the top of Fish Bay Road. The midday sun beat down, searing the seats of the jeep.

"No, sweetie. Let's just get this over with. I think the kids are at school. I really do," Sam said, leaning down to tuck into the jeep. He put the keys in the ignition and blasted the air conditioner to max. "Sorry, I should have come out and started this up before so you wouldn't get so hot."

She loved him for wanting her to be as comfortable as she could be when they went to talk to Neil about why they had come to St. John. She had been holding it all in for so long that it would be a relief to finally share her story. But Deirdre felt a wave of hesitation, reminding her of that odd moment when she'd first gone into labor after nine eternal months of pregnancy. After waiting for and wanting the delivery to come, just as the first contractions began, she'd wondered, is this really such a good idea?

Sam had shared his confidence in Neil Perry, telling Deirdre he was a man who could be trusted. Oh, he was a bit of a rogue, to be sure, but he was also a man of integrity. Sam seemed certain. The Rankin case proved it. Deirdre trusted Sam, so she should trust Neil, she told herself.

Sam had to park in the lot at St. John Car Rental, the lot at Bar None being full. He took Deidre's hand as they crossed the street and approached Bar None, which was fairly full after an afternoon shower.

Sam approached the bartender who had served them their first drink on the island the day they arrived and asked if Neil was there. Mitch wouldn't comment until Sam told him why he wanted to talk to Neil. Sam explained he had information he thought would be helpful to Neil. Deirdre listened to the exchange, still feeling a sense of apprehension as if she were about to set off a chain of events over which she would have no control.

Neil came out of a corner booth, gesturing for Deirdre and Sam to enter.

"What can I do for you folks?" Neil asked, signaling to Deirdre this would be a short conversation. She noticed the booth was kind of a primitive office.

"Actually, we think we may be able to do something for you and your friends at Ten Villas," she said, surprising herself and probably Sam by taking the lead.

"Really?" Neil said, pointing to the bench on the other side of the booth where they could sit. "Can I offer you something to drink?"

Both Sam and Deirdre settled for lemonade.

"We need to disclose some information about the man who was murdered at Villa Mascarpone. We may also share it with the police, but we hoped you might give us your guidance after hearing us out," Sam said.

"So this isn't about the Rankin case?" Neil said.

"No, you were clear about that, Neil. May I call you Neil?" Sam said.

"Yes. So what do you mean by guidance? I generally don't give guidance anymore. I run a bar." Neil said, folding his hands in front of him on the table.

"Not legal advice. We have a lawyer, a good one back in Massachusetts," Deirdre said.

"We're really looking for guidance about how to approach a sensitive situation. We wondered who we should contact in law enforcement, given the circumstances," Sam said.

"And this is about Carter Johnson, right?" Neil asked.

"His real name is Joel Levin," Deirdre said.

"How did you hear that?" Neil sat up erect and at attention.

"Because he was working for me. I hired him a couple of years ago after he retired from the FBI." Deirdre emptied her glass of lemonade.

"He promised Deirdre he wouldn't quit looking until he found them," Sam said.

"Found who?"

Deirdre glanced at Sam, who nodded.

"Go ahead, honey. It's okay to tell him."

"My kids," Deirdre said, choking up. "He found them here on St. John."

"You have kids on St. John? I'm not sure I'm following you. Are you thinking the murder has something to do with finding your kids?"

"I don't know. All I know is that Joel came down to St. John to document what was necessary to pull in the FBI. We were to wait at Villa Mascarpone until the FBI arrived to retrieve the kids and bring charges. Of course, that never happened, which is why we're here," Deirdre said.

Neil waited a few seconds, rubbing his hand over his stubbly chin, and then leaned forward.

"Your kids, they're not Mara and Rory's twins? Are you kidding me?" Neil said.

"They are not Mara and Rory's twins, Neil. They are Robby Keegan's—now Rory Eagan—and my kids, Neil. They are not twins. And, no, I am not kidding you."

"How long have you been looking for your kids?"

"Thirteen years. Here's the paperwork," Deirdre said, sliding a thick file across the table.

Neil sifted through the papers. Deirdre noticed him placing official documents in a pile: her divorce decree, the kids' birth certificates, Robby's old passport, the habeas corpus writ demanding he return the children to the Commonwealth of Massachusetts that had never been served on him. Finally, he looked up at Deirdre.

"Well, Deirdre. Thirteen years is a long time to wait for what's rightfully yours. Let's get over to Lee Janquar and finish the job Joel Levin started."

Chapter Thirty-Nine

Mara got into the car and pounded her fists on the dashboard. Sabrina turned on the ignition, knowing they couldn't get out of there fast enough. Janquar was taking Rory and Tanya to the police station where the "conversation" would continue. He had politely requested that Mara join them. The only good out of this latest development was that at least Sabrina wasn't the one currently in the hot seat. Oh, but she felt for Mara.

"I cannot believe that Rory would stoop so low as to sneak a woman into the home he shares with his children. How long has this been going on?"

Sabrina knew there was little a friend could offer in the way of words. She knew her job was to listen. She was finally getting this friendship thing down.

"I am done, I am so done. I thought I could put up with him for the children through the next two years 'til they went to college, but no way can we put up with this," Mara said. "He is such a pig." She finally burst into sobs.

Sabrina was tempted to pull over to the side of the road but thought better of it when she remembered that Janquar and company would be coming along soon. She wouldn't give Rory Eagan the satisfaction of seeing what he had done to the wife he didn't deserve.

"Mara, I'm so sorry you're going through this," Sabrina said and suddenly realized that her problems weren't necessarily as cataclysmic as she had thought.

"I feel like such a fool. I know everyone here on the island thinks I am the village idiot because I put up with him and his womanizing. I'm sure they think I tolerate him because I'm an unattractive woman who landed a stud of a husband. But they're wrong, Sabrina, dead wrong, and not just about the stud thing. He had me trapped. He wouldn't let me adopt the children so he would always have a hold on me. 'Throw me out and you'll never see those kids again.' The miserable excuse for a father," Mara said, shaking the hand with which she had given Rory a small dose of what he deserved.

"Does it hurt?" Sabrina asked.

Mara laughed. "Yes, but I feel better than I have in years. The pain in my hand might be worth it."

They arrived at the police headquarters to find the same desk sergeant on duty. This time Sabrina took note of his name on his badge and greeted him properly.

"Good afternoon, Officer Milan. Detective Janquar asked Ms. Bennett to meet him here," Sabrina said, giving Mara a little more time to collect herself.

"Yes, he called ahead. He asked if you would please have a seat and wait for him," he said, pointing to a large waiting area with orange benches arranged in a square. A plastic table sat in the middle, with a copy of the *Tradewinds*, the weekly island newspaper, and a pot of plastic flowers on top.

Sabrina picked up the newspaper and handed it to Mara. "Here. If you have to sit in the same room with him, you can at least avoid looking at him from behind the newspaper."

The door opened, letting a rush of warm air in, although Sabrina could hear it was raining. To her surprise, Deirdre Leonard entered followed by her husband and Neil, who pulled the door shut. Deirdre shook raindrops from her hair and walked over to the benches.

"Why, hello," she said to Sabrina and Mara as if they'd run into each other at a doctor's office. But Deirdre didn't seem quite as self-assured as she had yesterday when she'd arrived at Villa Mascarpone.

"Hello," Sabrina said, wondering exactly how much weirder one day could get. What were they doing here? Why was Neil with them? What was in the bulging file folder with the six-inch gusset wrapped with a cord, she wondered. Was this the "situation" that made him too busy to talk to her on the phone? Neil nodded to her as he walked over to the counter.

"Good afternoon," Mara said, and then dove behind the *Tradewinds*.

Deirdre and Sam sat on a bench perpendicular to Mara and Sabrina.

Sabrina heard Neil tell the desk officer he was here to see Detective Janquar on important business relating to the death of Carter Johnson. He had information related to Carter Johnson's death and he was handing it over to the cops without even cluing her in? Sabrina was outraged. What was going on here?

"Better take a number, Mr. Perry. Detective Janquar is expected shortly but there are other folks ahead of you," Office Milan said politely.

Chapter Forty

Liam and Kelly sat next to each other on the ferry. While they attended the same school, their teachers had strongly advised against placing twins in the same classes, which they feared would breed too much competition, so they hadn't had a chance to catch up until now.

Kelly knew Liam's team had won the swim meet. She also knew he was dreading going home. They knew pretty much everything about each other. She had told Liam about her relationship with Seth long before she had told any of the girls at school.

"You can't imagine how awful Dad was with Seth, Liam, and in front Mara and Henry and everyone else on the beach," Kelly said, filling Liam in on the disastrous day he had missed.

"Wait 'til he finds out I'm gay. That day will top them all," Liam said.

"Then don't tell him. Wait 'til you're at college to come out. He's so mean about Henry. You can't want him talking about you like that," Kelly said as the ferry hit a wave, causing her and Liam to grasp their backpacks.

"No. I am gay, Kelly. That's who I am. I know that now. I've waded through the confusion. I'm going to tell Mara first and see what she suggests about telling Dad," Liam said.

"Not tonight, Liam. Mara's had a rough couple of days. Everyone is still all balled up about that guy getting killed. Maybe you should ask Henry about it when he picks us up. You'll have time with him alone, because I'm going to surprise Seth and go to his apartment," Kelly said, a big smile on her face.

"Does Mara know this?" Liam asked.

"Of course not, silly. But she'll have to get used to the idea if I decide to move in with Seth, won't she? I just can't live at home with Dad anymore, Liam. I just can't."

"I know it's bad, really I do. But you don't know Seth well enough to move in with him."

"I know him well enough to have sex with him, don't I?"

Liam had been the one to persuade her to go to the clinic in St. Thomas and get birth control pills when she'd made it clear she wanted a "complete" relationship with Seth.

"He won't even tell you exactly how old he is, Kelly. Come on, you know that's not right."

The ferry slowed down as Cruz Bay emerged from the distance. Kelly could see people at the dock. She hoped Henry would be distracted with picking up guests he had to take to a villa so she could slip away. She planned to walk up to Seth's apartment and spend a few hours with him before Mara or Henry caught up with her. Liam would cover for her. That's what twins did for each other.

They got off the ferry, dodging the tourists heavily laden with luggage they wouldn't need.

"I don't see Henry, do you?" asked Liam, looking around at the vehicles squished into the tiny parking area.

"Nope. Time for me to go. Talk to Henry about how to break the news. He'll know what to do," Kelly said, pecking her brother's cheek before ducking into the crowd.

Chapter Forty-One

Sabrina jolted upright when the door next to the counter where the desk officer sat opened. Leon Janquar poked his head through, opening the door for Rory Eagan to enter from behind him. Rory skulked in after scanning the room. Mara had landed him quite the shiner.

"Here you go, Mr. Eagan. I need you to sit over on the bench across from Mr. Perry. No need for you to be sitting near your wife," Janquar said.

"Lee, I have some urgent news about the investigation," Neil said, rising to move toward the detective, still clutching the oversized file.

"Neil, I'll get to you as soon as I can, but like they say on TV, I've got breaking events here. Everybody behave for Officer Milan, and I'll get to you as soon as I'm done talking to Tanya," Janquar said, stepping back through the door.

"No, no, you don't understand, Lee. You can't leave these people all out here," Neil said, but the door had shut. Neil looked over at the young officer at the desk, who simply shrugged.

Sabrina remained astounded. Why was Neil behaving so oddly? She was tempted to ask him to step outside for a word, but she couldn't leave Mara alone now that Rory was in the waiting room. Mara was clenching and unclenching her right fist, which Sabrina could see was progressively swelling.

She saw Neil look over at Mara's hand.

"I hope everything's okay with you," Neil said to Mara.

"I'll get over it," Mara said.

Sabrina noticed Sam Leonard clutching his wife's hand. Why weren't the happy vacationers at the beach instead of at the local police station holding hands like they were watching a scary movie? Deirdre was looking down at her sandals. No one was talking.

"You'll be lucky if I don't press charges against you and take out a restraining order," Rory said from across the table between him and Mara.

Uh-oh, Sabrina thought, here we go. She saw Deirdre Leonard look up from the floor and gaze over at Rory. Deirdre's nostrils flared as a red blotchiness covered her neck. The curse of being a redhead, Sabrina thought. Your skin gives you away.

"So someone beat me to it," Deirdre said, her voice rising. She was on her feet, storming over toward Rory.

"Excuse me?" he said, noticing her move toward him.

"Deirdre, wait, please. Let Neil handle this," Sam said, jumping out of his chair, taking Deirdre by the arm.

Neil stepped toward Deirdre. "Folks, let's just—"

"You thought you would get away with it? How dare you take those kids from me! Who gave you the right to play God, to change their identities, their lives? How could you do that to your own children—to *my* children?" Deirdre collapsed, sobbing into the arms of her husband who had rushed to her side.

"Dee?" Rory Eagan rose from his bench looking terrified at the woman who wept uncontrollably.

"Dee? Dee? Rory?" Mara leapt off the bench around the table and over to her husband.

"Rory?" Mara screamed this time.

The door opened as Lyla Banks entered.

"Mara, are you all right?" Lyla asked.

"No, not Rory, Robby," Deirdre said, turning to Mara.

"Robby? Who's Robby?" Mara asked Deirdre first, and then she turned to Rory. "Who the hell is Robby?"

"Robby Keegan, my former husband. The father of my children, Liam and Kelly Keegan. Not Liam and Kelly Eagan, and not your children, Mara. My children. Oh, how clever you were to change their last name so close to the one they were born to, Robby. Little kids, traumatized by the abrupt removal of their mother from their lives could be convinced of anything, couldn't they, Robby?" Deirdre was no longer crying. Her voice had grown in strength and volume as Mara shrunk in horror.

"The car accident, the suicide?" Mara asked.

"All lies. He abducted them. It's all here," Sam said, pointing to the folder Neil still clutched.

"Neil?" Mara asked, looking desperate for a different answer.

"It's true. There's documentation here, which makes it seem irrefutable. I'm sorry, Mara," Neil said.

"You son of a bitch," Mara said to Rory. "How could you do this to those children, to her, to me?"

Neil stepped between Mara and Rory, who was huddled over in a corner, with his back turned to the lynch mob. Then Rory rushed to the counter.

"I demand police protection from these insane women," he said.

Neil stood behind Rory. Sabrina knew he was making certain the women he wronged didn't attack him as he insisted the desk officer get Janquar. Now Sabrina understood why Neil was acting so strange. The Leonards had obviously asked him to act as their liaison with local law enforcement. Once Neil heard their plight, he had to have agonized over how this would affect people he knew and cared for on St. John. Oh, what a mess.

"Mr. Eagan, you heard Detective Janquar. Have a seat and be patient. No one is going to hurt you in a police station, sir," Office Milan said in a tone that Sabrina understood meant "Don't mess with me." Sabrina wished she were as confident as Officer Milan seemed to be that one or both of the two women Rory Eagan had betrayed wouldn't add to the injury Mara had already inflicted. Even though he deserved it, Sabrina knew it would only make things worse. But then again, she didn't think things really could get worse.

That was, until Lyla Banks stepped around Neil and up to the counter and said, "Officer, I'm sorry to interrupt, but I need to report a stolen gun."

Chapter Forty-Two

Kelly walked up the long, narrow winding road, which climbed at such an angle that it was almost perpendicular. Great for the inner thighs, she kept telling herself.

She'd done all her homework in school so she and Seth could enjoy the little time they had with each other. He didn't know she was coming, but she knew what time he came home from pool cleaning each day because he always called her.

She had been invited to his place many times and even knew he kept a key under a concrete frog statue next to the door mat, but she'd never had the opportunity to grab a couple of hours like this.

At the top of the hill, she found Seth's small apartment building and went around back until she saw unit C. She looked around for the frog, finally finding it hiding under an overgrown lipstick plant. She lifted up and found the key.

Kelly unlocked the door, wishing she had brought some beer or at least a snack. It was bad manners not to come with a little gift the first time.

Inside, the apartment was dark, shades drawn down, and it smelled of chlorine and sweat combined. She didn't care. This was where Seth lived. Where she might live if they decided to be together on St. John.

Kelly looked at her cell phone. It would be at least another half hour before Seth arrived home. She reached into her backpack and took out a spare pair of shorts and a tank top she had packed from her locker. She folded her uniform neatly and tucked it into her backpack. Mara was wrong. She really was organized.

But Seth was a bit of a slob. She supposed this was the way of most boys. Kelly began picking up a little bit here and there. She made a pile of what she assumed was dirty laundry, taking much of it off the mattress on the floor, which served as Seth's bed. She straightened the covers and puffed the pillows. She picked up some surf magazines, making sure the corners were aligned. Mara always said, "If you have to have piles in your room, Kelly, at least make neat ones."

The place was beginning to look pretty good until Kelly stepped into the tiny bathroom. The sink definitely needed some kind of miracle in a spray bottle. Kelly walked over to the small kitchen, noting that countertop fridge and tiny stove also were grimy. The sink was no better. She saw a cabinet beneath it and opened the door. She found a cleaner called Wowzie and an old sponge next to it. As she reached in to grab the sponge, her hand touched something cool and smooth. She lifted it and pulled it out. She was holding a gun, she realized, and almost dropped it out of fear. Kelly looked back in and saw a large camera and a backpack. She pulled them out, her heart pounding, not knowing why she didn't just get up and run.

This was not good, she knew. Liam's words, warning her that she didn't know Seth all that well, rang in her ears. Kelly was stunned to learn that you could be having sex with someone, could know the nooks and crannies of his body, but not have a clue about what was under his kitchen counter or in his head.

She figured she'd better learn what she didn't know about Seth. Kelly unzipped the main compartment to the backpack and pulled out several large stiff envelopes. She opened one to find two pieces of cardboard sandwiching a pile of photos. Photos of her house, her road, Mara's car, her father's car. Photos of the Banks' house and their car. There were a couple of photos looking out at Ram Head. But from where? She shivered as she realized these shots had been taken from Villa Mascarpone.

Kelly opened the next two envelopes and found photos of her, Liam, Mara, and her father. Why was someone taking so many pictures of her family and the Bankses, although there were only a few of them?

She looked on the fronts of the envelopes. They were all addressed to Deirdre Leonard in South Hadley, Massachusetts.

The pictures were weird, but the gun terrified her. Why did Seth have all this stuff? Should she call Henry and have him come get her? Kelly saw a third thick envelope and decided she should see what was in it before panicking.

She heard the doorknob turn and saw Seth's surprised expression as she stayed sitting on the floor, everything laid out around her: the gun, the envelopes, the camera, and backpack.

"Babe?" he said, closing the door behind him.

"I thought I'd surprise you," Kelly said, knowing she had shocked him. "Seth, what's with all of this stuff?"

"I can explain, Kelly. I just wanted to wait for the right time," he said, placing his own backpack on the floor.

"I think that this is about as good a time as we're going to get."

"Kelly, trust me. I haven't done anything wrong. Honestly. I just have some things to tell you about yourself that you don't know about. I didn't want to upset you. How much time do we have? Can we head up to our special spot on Ram Head? It's stopped raining," Seth said, coming over and sitting next to Kelly.

"Maybe a couple of hours," Kelly said, feeling the warmth spread throughout her body as Seth kissed her neck.

"Perfect. Let's head out while there's still plenty of light," Seth said, grabbing the backpack on the floor, stuffing the envelopes, camera, and gun back inside.

"Why do you need those?" Kelly asked, picking up her own backpack, reaching to place her cell phone in her shorts pocket.

"You'll see. It's part of what I need to talk to you about. Don't worry, I'm going to take care of you," Seth said as he led her to his scooter.

Chapter Forty-Three

Henry enjoyed having Liam's company while he transported guests from the ferry to their villas. Sometimes he missed being with people like he had been when he worked for the airlines. He and Liam dropped the last group of guests at their villa and headed back to Cruz Bay.

Henry had been happy to share his experiences with Liam about coming out with his own family and how some of his friends had handled it. He suggested Liam talk to a counselor before he made any announcement, if for no other reason than he would have professional support from a therapist no matter how it went down.

"Time to pick up your sister, Liam. Want to give her a call on your cell and tell her the party's over?" Kelly had been considerate to find something else to do so Liam would be able to talk to him one on one. Liam had his sister in his corner, and Henry was sure Mara would be supportive too.

Liam made the call to Kelly while Henry waited, parked near Bar None.

"She's not picking up," Liam said, a look of concern coming over his face.

"Do you know where she is?"

"Um," Liam said, shifting in his seat.

"Come on, come clean," Henry said.

"Seth's, but don't say I told you, please."

"No problemo. I know where Seth lives. I've delivered his check there once or twice. Let's do a little surveillance," Henry said.

Henry drove the van up the steep road that led to Seth's apartment, swinging around back to see if Seth's scooter was there. No scooter.

He picked up his cell phone and dialed Seth's number. No answer.

Henry got out, went up to the apartment, and knocked.

No answer here, either. He didn't like this. Kelly had been his responsibility, even if she had taken off before he'd had the chance to pick her up.

He tried opening the door, but it was locked. Running a vacation villa business where guests were always losing keys made Henry suspect there was what he called a "hidey-hole." He looked around, noticed the concrete frog, which was what sat on the steps of at least half the inhabitants of the island, and found the key.

He looked over at Liam, who sat in the van looking uncomfortable.

When he opened the door, Henry was surprised to see how neat Seth's place was. Having a girlfriend must've improved his housekeeping habits. Henry called out, "Inside, Henry looking for Seth and Kelly," but there was no answer. That's when he saw the fancy telephoto Nikon D750 lens cap on the floor, the same cap for the lens he had seen on Carter Johnson's camera when he'd delivered appetizers to him. He picked up the lens cap with his handkerchief and placed it in his pocket.

He backed out of the apartment, deciding not to touch anything else. He had a very bad feeling, which he tried to hide as he got back in the van.

"They must be off somewhere. Got any idea where so we can retrieve your sister before she gets in trouble with Mara?" Henry asked as casually as he could.

"Not really," said Liam. "Unless they hiked out to Ram Head."

Chapter Forty-Four

"All right, what do we have here? Officer Milan tells me we're about to have mayhem," Leon Janquar said as he pressed forward into the waiting room. Sabrina knew Milan must have pushed a panic button of sorts because he'd never picked up a phone or let his eyes leave the room.

"I'm just trying to report a stolen gun, Detective," Lyla Banks said in her best matriarch voice.

"That man stole my children. I want him arrested for kidnapping," Deirdre said, standing and pointing to Rory Eagan.

"He probably killed Carter Johnson, the investigator we hired to find the children," Sam added.

"The hell I did. It was probably that old geezer who's perpetually trimming bushes. He was out there that morning. Showed me a photo the tourist had taken. I'm surprised he didn't chop him up instead of shooting him," Rory said to Janquar.

"You miserable excuse for a man. How dare you make unfounded accusations like that about my husband when you're nothing but a drunken, crude, miserable husband and father," Lyla said, stepping toward Rory, but not before Leon Janquar filled the space between them.

"Okay, folks, we're going to have to simmer down here. Do you have any evidence showing Mr. Eagan kidnapped your kids, ma'am? Do you know where they are now?"

Neil turned to Janquar, handing him the folder.

"It's all here, Lee. It looks legit. It seems Mr. Eagan, a.k.a. Robert Keegan, fled Massachusetts some thirteen years ago with his two children from a former marriage with this woman, now Deirdre Leonard. He simply never returned them from a visit and vanished with them until now. Deirdre Leonard is the mother of Liam and Kelly Keegan, not Eagan," Neil said, gesturing toward Deirdre, who had now become very quiet and pale.

"She spent thirteen years searching for them. Carter Johnson, whose real name is Joel Levin, finally found them for us after all of these years. We feel awful about what happened to him," Sam said, putting his arm around Deirdre.

"I have never stopped looking for my children. Never. Robby has stolen something no one can ever replace. They deserved to be raised by their mother, not to be told lies about her. He told them I was a drunk who drove into a tree because I couldn't handle being their mother. They must have believed I didn't love them enough to want to raise them. What a horrible legacy to hand to your children. They aren't even twins, but school records show he's raised them to think they are," Deirdre said, pointing toward Rory with her index finger, like a lawyer arguing to a jury. Sabrina admired the ferocity of Deirdre's love for her children. What would life have been like for her if she'd had a mother who loved her enough to stay instead of running away?

"Oh, no you don't. You were a terrible mother, a lush, not competent enough to raise a puppy, let alone my two kids. I saved them from you. Look at how wonderful they turned out," Rory said, turning on Deirdre.

"I was a good mother, Robby, and you knew it. You didn't take them from me because I was a drunk or a lousy mother. You took them from me because I dared to divorce you, to end your tyranny over me and two little kids, who cowered when you came home after being out drinking and sleeping around. You thought you were in charge and when I said, 'No more. I don't have to accept this kind of behavior,' you snapped. You aren't responsible for how lovely the children are, Robby. She is," Deirdre said, looking over at Mara.

"Mr. Eagan, it looks like we need to have another conversation now. I have to warn you, if what this woman is saying is true, we're going to be having a little visit from the FBI," Janquar said, opening the door to the back of the station once again.

"Wait, she knows I didn't do anything to that man at Villa Mascarpone. She was with me that whole morning,"

Rory said, looking over at Tanya, who had entered the room without Sabrina noticing. She was standing as far away from the group in the room as you could without exiting. She looked pale, and Sabrina knew she was just a one-way ticket away from going back to Texas. She certainly didn't have a job at Ten Villas anymore.

"Mr. Eagan," Janquar said, indicating Rory should come with him.

"Wait, I want a lawyer. Mara, call one of your lawyers to get over here, right now," Rory said, moving slowly toward Janquar.

"Get your own lawyer. For the kidnapping and the divorce."

Neil looked at Sabrina, his blue eyes fixing on hers in a knowing way. Neither of them was good at handling human emotion and this was a whole ocean of it. She sensed he might be unraveling and reached over for his hand, squeezing it.

"You're okay, Salty. You're okay," he whispered.

"So are you, Neil. You are doing fine," she said.

The relief was palpable once Rory Eagan exited the room.

Tanya walked over to Mara, tears running down her face.

"I pray you will forgive me, ma'am."

Mara said nothing, just nodded.

"My husband may be ill, but he didn't harm anyone. Someone stole our gun," Lyla said, piping up once more to no one in particular.

"I'm sure this will all get sorted out, Lyla," Neil said.

Maybe, Sabrina thought, but how? Where was their gun? Who had killed Carter Johnson? What would happen to Kelly and Liam?

Sabrina heard the door to the entrance of the police station open behind Neil and her and wondered, Dear God, who and what now?

"What's going on? Why is everyone here?" Sabrina heard Henry ask and turned to find him entering with Liam. Mara rose immediately, seeming to sense trouble, and moved toward Liam. Deirdre remained seated, her eyes fixed on the son she hadn't seen in more than a decade. Sabrina ached for her. She couldn't imagine ever having children, but if she did and someone ripped them from her arms, well, she didn't want to think about what she might do.

"Henry? Liam? Where's Kelly" Mara asked, panic in her voice.

"We're not sure, Mara. We think she's with Seth, maybe hiking out to Ram Head," Henry said.

"How stupid can she be?" Mara said, raising her eyes up to the heavens. No, Sabrina thought, she wouldn't have made a good mother at all. She would be the kind of mother ready to wring Kelly's little neck for being so dumb about men.

"We checked Seth's apartment—that's where she said she was going—but they weren't there," Liam said.

"But this was," Henry said, pulling the telephoto camera lens cap from his pocket with a tissue. "I'm sure this cap was part of Carter Johnson's fancy camera equipment, the stuff I saw out at Villa Mascarpone. I came right here once I realized—"

"Oh my god," Mara said.

"Oh, no," Deirdre said.

"I've got to go to her," Mara said.

"Me too," Deirdre said.

"Just wait a minute while I get Lee," Neil said.

"I'm not waiting for anyone. I won't lose Kelly again," Deirdre said, moving toward the door, Sam two steps behind her.

"I'll start driving them out in the van, Neil. You and Janquar can catch up with us," Sabrina said, grabbing the keys from Henry.

"Sam, will you stay with Liam and Henry, please?" Deirdre asked in what Sabrina knew was Deirdre's first maternal command of what would become many.

"Sure, I'll fill Henry in," he said.

"Who are all these people?" Liam asked Henry.

"We're all your people, Liam. Yours and Kelly's. You'll see," Sam said as he watched Deirdre, Mara, and Sabrina rush out the door.

Chapter Forty-Five

The hike out to Ram Head had taken a bit longer than usual, since the trail was still a little wet from the rain. Kelly watched the steam rise from the rocks on the portion of the hike her father always said reminded him of the beaches of New England. He had been a gentler dad when he and Mara had first gotten married, and they'd done things as a family. Kelly wasn't sure why her father always seemed so angry, but she was fairly sure the anger was what made him drink. She had given up hoping he would stop long ago. It was never going to happen and she knew it.

Seth seemed quiet. Kelly wanted to know what he had to tell her about herself. She wondered if he was going to break up with her, tell her she was immature. But what was with the gun?

They climbed the final ascent toward Ram Head, the breeze beginning to build. The view from the last cliff before Ram Head was Kelly's favorite. Her father used to tell her that long ago, pirates had hidden in a crevice that sliced partway through the horrendously high cliff, and she had believed him.

Kelly knew it would be dark on the hike back, but she didn't mind. She'd done this trail so many times that she could probably do it asleep. She was more nervous about Mara's reaction to her sneaking out with Seth again. She was pushing her luck.

At the top of Ram Head, she took a swig of water and found a rock to sit on. Seth perched on one closer to the edge, one Kelly had favored as a child, always making Mara nervous.

"Come here, babe," Seth said, patting the spot next to him on the rock.

She rose, a little reluctantly and wasn't sure why. Waiting for him to tell her something made her very uncomfortable.

Kelly sat next to him and decided she could wait no longer.

"What is it that you want to tell me, Seth? I need to know."

"Well, it seems, Kelly, that everyone on this island has secrets. I know I do, and so do you," Seth said in a very calm voice, one Kelly hadn't heard before.

"I haven't got any secrets." She wondered if he thought she had another boyfriend over in St. Thomas, as he'd accused her of on several occasions. The guys at her high school were so immature compared to Seth. How could he imagine she would choose one of them over him?

"But you do. Your name is even a secret. Did you know your real last name is Keegan, not Eagan?"

"That's ridiculous." Kelly began to laugh but stopped when she saw the serious look in Seth's eyes. She wondered if it had been a huge mistake coming out here.

"You need to hear the truth. You have the right to know." Seth stood and faced her.

"Know what?" She was beginning to feel exasperated with Seth, who was towering over her as she sat crouched on a rock.

"Kelly, your real mother isn't dead. You and Liam aren't even twins. You were born eleven months before him. Your father made that up when he kidnapped you and Liam. The woman renting Villa Mascarpone is your real mother."

"What are you saying? None of this is true."

"But it is. It's all in the report the private investigator wrote. It's over there in his backpack. I found it the morning he was supposed to leave Villa Mascarpone, when I went to clean the pool. He was getting out of the pool and headed for the shower. He told me I could clean the pool but to be careful not to splash water on this camera equipment and backpack, which he had ready to go on one of the lounge chairs. I went to move them farther away and saw a folder marked 'FBI.' I was curious, and I could hear the shower running, so I took a peek. And it was a good thing for you and Liam that I did."

"I don't understand. What's the FBI got to do with this? I just don't get it." Kelly began to cry, wondering what had been in the envelope she had been about to open when Seth arrived at his apartment.

"I had to protect you. You were so sweet and young, different from other girls."

"Protect me from what?" Kelly asked, almost shrieking.

"He was going to send his report with pictures of you and Liam to the FBI, Kelly, because they have jurisdiction over kidnapping. Your father was going to be prosecuted and probably go to jail. You would have been sent away from St. John, away from me. I saved you from all of that. Can't you see that?"

"How did you save me? Seth, what have you done? Tell me." Kelly detected desperation in Seth's voice. Finding the backpack and other stuff in his apartment had been a huge mistake.

"Your real mother was going to take you to live in Massachusetts, so you and Liam would live with her happy little family. She was going to take you away from me. I had to take care of that situation and protect you."

"Seth, did you kill that man?" Kelly asked without thinking.

"Of course I did. I did it for you. I had no choice. Don't worry, I'm not going to get caught. I'm pretty sure they're going to blame Mr. Banks. I gave him one of the photographs taken by the dead guy. That Alzheimer's gets him pretty confused. He can't remember his own name. I mean, he hangs his gun in his shed next to his hedge trimmer. I'll toss the backpack and camera bag off the cliff. No one will ever find it."

"You can't let Mr. Banks go to jail for something you did. You have to go to the police. Tell them it was an accident. Tell them you didn't mean it. Please, Seth." Kelly rose to her feet, sobbing.

"I can't do that. They'd put me in jail, and we couldn't be together. The whole reason I did this was so we can be together. I did it because I love you, Kelly."

Kelly walked over to the spot where she'd dropped her backpack, slinging it over her shoulder.

"I have to go," she said, turning to face Seth, wondering how she ever had let him into her life.

"No, you can't leave me. I did it for you." Seth grabbed Kelly by the arm, pulling her toward him. Kelly's backpack fell to the ground, next to the one belonging to the man Seth had killed.

"Seth, let go. I can't be with you."

Kelly tried pulling away from him, but he was too strong. He yanked her arm to pull her back toward him and stumbled, losing his balance. Seth tried to steady himself, still holding onto her.

"Stop!" Kelly screamed, knowing they were too close to the edge. But it was too late. They tumbled backward over the edge, his screams and hers now one.

Chapter Forty-Six

Sabrina hit the van's gas pedal and sped out of the parking lot at police headquarters, not caring if a dozen police officers saw her. They would have to chase her to Ram Head before she'd stop. She had no idea how fast three women, followed by what she hoped would be a bunch of cops, could get out to Ram Head, but she didn't have time to think about it.

Deirdre sat in the front seat next to her, with Mara in the backseat in the middle so she could talk to them.

"What do you know about this Seth?" Deirdre asked.

"He's our pool guy at Ten Villas. Does a good job, responsible, but other than that, I don't know much," Sabrina said.

"He was our pool guy, but Rory fired him for paying too much attention to Kelly. I guess he was a little too late," Mara said.

Deirdre reached back with her hand, taking Mara's.

"That's not important now. We just need her to be safe. We'll sort the rest out later." Deirdre said.

"Absolutely," Mara said.

Sabrina was thrilled these two mothers weren't ready to kill each other because she was afraid Seth was more than the three of them could handle.

Sabrina wound over the hills and curves of Center-line Road at a speed that frightened even her. When they turned right at the signs for Coral Bay and headed toward Salt Pond, she found herself entering a state of calm she had been able to call upon since her childhood. Sabrina breathed with awareness, knowing there was a dangerous tendency to not breathe when a crisis arose, leaving one without the oxygen one needed more than ever. She listened while Mara described the hike out to Ram Head to Deirdre, preparing her for it, as she was the only one of the three of them who hadn't made the trek before. Sabrina wondered if Deirdre was the hiking type, thinking how delicate she looked, but was pleased to hear her say she and Sam hiked in the Berkshires all the time.

She slowed when she saw the "Dip" caution sign, which someone had added "Clam" above. Later at the speed "hump," as it was called in St. John, Sabrina slowed again, cursing the random speed humps, which were constructed by people in neighborhoods concerned about wild tourists who couldn't remember to "think left" when they were driving. Sabrina had hoped she could make good time driving to Salt Pond, knowing there wasn't much she could do to hasten the hike out to Ram Head.

"I used to dream of being reunited with Liam and Kelly," Deirdre said. "I just didn't expect she might be in danger."

"Can't you get this van to move a little faster, Sabrina?" Mara asked, sounding agitated to Sabrina after hearing Deirdre's concern. Sabrina felt it too.

Sabrina finally pulled into the parking lot at Salt Pond. There were no other cars, and she didn't see Seth's scooter, but he could have hidden it under the lush brush anywhere. It was still light but fading.

They were able to descend the long, wide path to Salt Pond Bay without much difficulty. Sabrina knew the ascent was the killer on the journey, but if they made it back safely with Kelly, it didn't matter.

They trotted along the fine white sand of the beach until they hit the trail on the other side. Deirdre and Sabrina were wearing flip-flops, but Mara was dressed in her sensible work boots, so she led the way. They climbed along the rocks and then up the clay hills along the water until they hit the rocky beach everyone agreed didn't belong there. It was so quintessential New England that people often suggested it was imported, but everyone knew it was just one of the natural surprises St. John offered. Deirdre and Sabrina had a little difficulty navigating the large gray rocks in flip-flops, but Mara held on to them and they passed through, reaching the final ascent.

They could see Ram Head in the distance, but it was too far away to see if there were people at the summit. Mara led the three of them along the path so narrow you could only go single file. Deirdre went next, with Sabrina last to keep her steady. They held hands like preschoolers holding a rope on a field trip. No one had much to say, other than "Watch your step" or "Down a bit here."

One of Sabrina's favorite things about Ram Head was the quiet. Oh, you might hear a bird or an occasional boat motor in the distance, but for the most part, there was silence.

Sabrina was relieved when they reached the marker left by some volunteers from Scituate, Massachusetts, who had spent a vacation clearing and cleaning the trail one year. That meant they were just steps from the summit. Still, not a sound. Mara fell back beside Deirdre as they stepped onto the flat top of Ram Head. Sabrina pulled ahead. She was not a mother waiting to see the fate of her child. She could be fearless for these two women who weren't.

Deirdre gasped and Sabrina looked back to see her pointing to a backpack up at the edge of the cliff.

Mara went white.

"It's Kelly's," she groaned.

Sabrina looked over to the side of it and saw another backpack, larger than Kelly's.

"Is it Seth's?" Mara asked.

"No, it's Carter Johnson's," she said.

"Please just go look, Sabrina," Deirdre said.

"Please?" Mara asked.

They wanted her to look over the edge of the cliff and tell them what they already knew: that Kelly and Seth had gone over the edge, in either a Romeo and Juliet scenario or some other unimaginable moment of drama. Sabrina didn't want to find two young bodies mangled against the rocks, but she was the best candidate for the job, so she did.

She edged over to the cliff, wanting to drop down on her belly because she so hated heights. She never came this close to the edge when she hiked here, but today she had no choice.

Sabrina saw him first, way down, face up at the base of the cliff, waves beginning to splash over him. She looked to the right to find Kelly and then to the left, but she didn't see her.

Sabrina caught a glimpse of Kelly's terrified face from the corner of her eye. Kelly was hanging on to a sharp rock about ten feet below. Her expression was transfixed. Her hands seemed tiny and her bare feet were hanging, just ready to drop.

"Kelly, Kelly, don't move. Just breathe. You're going to be fine. Give me one minute. Don't move, honey, just breathe," Sabrina said.

Sabrina backed off the cliff and took off her belt, placing the large key ring on the ground. Deirdre and Mara stood gaping at her.

Sabrina raised her index finger to her mouth signaling for them to be silent.

"She's hanging on to a rock. We can't startle her or she'll drop. Give me your tool belt, Mara. Help me buckle them together and see if I can pull her up," Sabrina whispered.

Mara took the small tools she carried off the belt first and put them next to Sabrina's key ring. She took Sabrina's belt and fastened the buckle to her own belt. The length of the two belts together was about six feet. Sabrina figured it wasn't long enough to reach Kelly even if she lay down on her belly and reached over. She ran over to Carter's backpack and removed the nylon strap, making it as long as it would extend before attaching to the two belts with the buckle. Sabrina tugged to see if the two belts and strap would separate under Kelly's weight. Mara handed her a couple of carabiners from the pile of tools to strengthen the buckles.

"I want you to come over here and each take one of my legs and hold on to it for dear life," Sabrina said, now understanding where the expression came from.

Sabrina got down on her belly, feeling the dirt and pebbles against her legs, and dropped the belts over. It didn't reach near enough for Kelly to grip. Sabrina moved on her belly again closer to the edge, Mara and Deirdre inching with her. The sun was beginning to set over beyond St. Thomas, and Sabrina knew it would be dark within ten minutes. This had to work.

The belts dangled just above the rock where Kelly's hands clung. Sabrina could feel the might of each mother holding onto her legs as she wiggled down over the edge and spoke in almost a lullaby.

"Kelly, I want you to take the belt with one hand and then grab the rock again. Can you do that, sweetie? Hand up fast, grab the belt, and then back to the rock."

Kelly looked up at Sabrina, who knew they could lose her in this one move. But the only other choice was to let her drop from fatigue.

"Ready?"

She looked at Sabrina directly, and Sabrina knew that meant she was.

"Grab the belt and press it to the rock, got it?"

Kelly took her right hand and swiftly reached for the belt, clasping it back on the rock.

"Good, now take a couple of nice deep breaths. You're doing great," Sabrina said, feeling the fatigue in her thighs as Mara and Deirdre held them with ferocity.

"Now, Kelly, we're going to put your other hand above the one holding the belt and you're going to grab the belt above. Got it? Sweetie, take a deep breath and grab," Sabrina said, the blood beginning to rush to her head from leaning over the edge.

Kelly did it quickly, but Sabrina could see her sway a little with fatigue. They had to get her up quick while Kelly—and they—had the energy.

"Okay, next I want you to let go of the rock, holding on tightly to the belt and bringing your feet toward the cliff. You can do this, sweetie, I know you can," Sabrina said, not really sure if it was true. But she could feel that the mother-force holding on to her legs had faith, and it bolstered her own.

Sabrina watched the beautiful muscles in Kelly's arms, strong from years of tennis and swimming, flex as she grabbed the belt and let go of the rock, swaying first out away from the cliff and then toward it, resting her feet against the crumbling clay.

"Now you're going to walk up while we pull you, Kelly, but keep holding the belt every step."

Kelly moved one foot up and then the next, but her toes slid down as stones and bits of clay began to crumble.

"I can't. I'm scared!" Kelly screamed, the first words she had spoken since they had arrived.

"Listen to me, Kelly. 'I, Kelly, am not afraid. I, Kelly, am fearless.'"

"I can't."

"Just say it."

"I, Kelly, am not afraid. I, Kelly, am fearless."

Kelly took another step and this time didn't slip.

"I, Kelly, am not afraid. I, Kelly, am fearless," Kelly began chanting. Step by step, Kelly climbed the cliff, Sabrina's body holding on to the belts, the bodies of Kelly's mothers holding onto Sabrina.

Sabrina felt someone next to her on her right and saw Neil and then to her left where Leon Janquar was lying. Janquar and Neil were each able to grab hold of one of Kelly's arms and pull her up onto Sabrina's back. She could hear sobs coming from Kelly, from Mara and Deirdre, and from her. They lay in a human heap of exhaustion and triumph, not moving.

Janquar took control.

"I want everyone to stay just as you are now. Please do not move. We are so close to the edge that it might give way under the weight, so let's disengage slowly," Janquar said.

He had Deirdre and Mara back up first. They then helped pull Kelly to her feet, where she fell into Mara's arms. Sabrina then sidled back over the dirt until she was far enough away from the edge and it was safe to stand.

Neil and Janquar finally stood and looked at the four women, so dirty in the near dark that they were almost impossible to see.

Over by the trail marker stood Lucy Detree and half a dozen male officers. Before Sabrina knew it, Lucy was collecting the T-shirts from the male officers with her and bringing them over to Kelly, whose shirt was torn, and to the three shivering women.

Mara held Kelly in her arms while Deirdre looked on, obviously wanting to do the same. Sabrina walked over and put her arm around her.

"It will take time, Deirdre, but at least now you have it," Sabrina said.

Chapter Forty-Seven

The hike to the parking lot at Salt Pond Bay was easy after the literal cliffhanger they'd been through. Sabrina watched Kelly walk arm in arm with Mara, while she stayed a little behind with Deirdre.

Janquar insisted Kelly get checked out at the Myrah Keating Smith Clinic. He suggested that while they were there, Mara might want to have her hand examined. The one she'd clocked her husband with what seemed like a century ago.

"Come with us," Mara said, turning to Deirdre.

"Are you sure?" Deirdre asked.

"It's okay. I know. At least, I know what Seth told me," Kelly said, looking a little dazed. "Before he almost killed me," she added, beginning to sob.

Lucy Detree swept them into a cruiser and off to the clinic.

Sabrina stood with Neil and Janquar, chilled by an evening breeze and sore in her shoulders and thighs, but other than that, none the worse for wear.

"You did a great job getting that girl up the cliff, Ms. Salter. You saved her life," Janquar said.

"Why, thank you, Detective Janquar."

"Please, call me Lee," he said, extending his hand.

"And I am Sabrina," she said, shaking it heartily.

"And I am Neil, and you were wonderful, Salty. You are one helluva woman, but I never want to see you that close to the edge of a cliff again," Neil said, sweeping her into a huge hug, hurting her shoulders a little but not enough for Sabrina to make him stop.

Sabrina heard the police radio through one of the cruisers. Apparently, the police boat had managed to find Seth's body. The backpack with the gun and camera had been retrieved from the top of Ram Head.

"Seth was far more troubled than I would have guessed," Sabrina said to Neil.

"We'll find out all of that and more by the time we're done," Janquar said as he walked them over to the Ten Villas van.

"But it's good to know none of our St. John people, you or Mr. Banks or even Mr. Eagan, killed anyone," Janquar continued.

"What about Rory Eagan and the kids?" Sabrina asked.

"That's up to Massachusetts," Neil said.

"And Mrs. Leonard," Janquar added.

"I feel bad for those kids having to face what their father did," Neil said.

"Well, it won't be easy for them," said Sabrina, "but I can tell you between those two mothers, they're going to be just fine."

Chapter Forty-Eight

Sabrina refused to give any interviews about the murder at Villa Mascarpone and the rescue on Ram Head. Instead, she focused on what Neil had dubbed the "Cliffhanger Celebration."

The celebration took place over at Hawksnest Beach, where Sabrina and Henry covered the picnic tables with floral twin flat sheets they borrowed from their villas, placing bowls of bougainvillea on each one. It was a typical island party where everyone brought their favorite dish. Sabrina brought lemon tarragon shrimp.

Since she thought she might be falling in love with Neil, Sabrina was nervous about the conversation she knew she had to have with him. She knew they had reached a point where there could be no more secrets if there was ever to be trust between them.

She walked by the table where Mara and the kids were sitting on one bench, with Sam and Deirdre on the opposite.

Liam's plate was filled high with Sabrina's shrimp, which pleased her.

"Tell me more about swim team," Sam asked Liam, while Mara explained to Deirdre how much the children enjoyed their occasional trips to New York and that she was sure they'd love New England. Sabrina knew Deirdre, Sam, and Mara had engaged a mediator on-island to help them sort how to share the children and to help them through the reconfiguration of a tender new family. Deirdre had confided to Sabrina how relieved she was that the kids seemed to accept her into their lives, but she'd acknowledged how fiercely loyal they were to Mara. Sabrina expected they would spend summers and school breaks in Massachusetts with Deirdre and Sam and probably attend college there.

No one seemed to miss the man who made the party possible, the man who had stolen his own children and robbed them of a life with their biological mother. Rory was back in Massachusetts, probably having his own little pity party with lawyers, DAs, and cops. The laughter coming from the children and the women at the table was lighter than any she had ever heard while Rory was in the picture.

Sabrina felt a little hollow observing the "mothers," as she liked to call them, who had agreed that the kids couldn't have enough love and decided to share and care for them generously without being divisive. This was the price she paid for opting out of motherhood.

But that didn't mean she couldn't have love in her life. She looked over at Neil standing over the grill, placing a double burger on a bun for Lee Janquar, who had come with some of his officers to join in the celebration.

Gradually, the partygoers left as darkness began to fall and the no-see-ums joined them. Henry pulled off the last bed sheet from a table, took the bowl of flowers, and placed them in a box.

"I'm going to take these over to Lyla and Evan with some of the leftovers," Henry said, getting into the van. They had declined the invitation because Evan needed a little quiet time, Lyla explained.

And then it was just Sabrina and Neil, sitting at a picnic table with Girlfriend at their feet.

"Ready for your swim?" Neil asked, pulling a couple of towels out of a canvas bag.

"Sure," Sabrina said, surprised at Neil's memory of her routine with Girlfriend and even more pleased he had thought enough about it to bring towels.

She slipped off her sundress, under which she was wearing her bathing suit. She called Girlfriend and dove into the still warm water on Hawksnest Beach, relaxing more with each stroke she made toward the beach at Gibney, the stress of the events washing off her, her breathing the only sound in her ears. She didn't bother getting out of the water at Gibney, where she remembered the silly crew from INN trapped overnight behind the locked gate and smiled. Neil had been brilliant that night.

264 | C. Michele Dorsey

She moved a little faster as she reversed her swim back toward Hawksnest and Neil, ever aware of the four-legged creature, her friend swimming beside her. When she arrived back at Hawksnest, she found Neil nearly asleep floating on his back.

"Back so soon?" he asked, reaching for her hand as he led her out of the water and grabbed a towel, throwing it over her shoulders.

"Why didn't you tell me about what had happened to you in LA, Neil? We could have commiserated," Sabrina said.

"Salty, you were so skittish, I didn't dare show any flaws," Neil said. "Besides, after our little drunken swim when you first arrived on island, I knew I really liked you."

He lowered the towel from her right shoulder, leaning in and kissing her neck.

"You are just the right combinations of sweet and salty," he said, moving in a little closer.

Sabrina leaned in toward Neil as Girlfriend sank down onto the sand, knowing the party wasn't quite over.

Acknowledgments

My deepest gratitude to my talented and unflappable agent, friend, and fellow yogi, Paula Munier, and to Gina Panettieri, fearless leader of Talcott Notch Literary Agency. I am grateful to my editor, Matt Martz, at Crooked Lane Books along with his assistant, Nike Power, for their enthusiasm and patient nurturing.

I have had incredible support on my long and winding writing path, starting with my writing group, Women Who Write, and, in particular, from Christine "Cissy" White. My fellow Sisters in Crime New England have been more than inspirational. I have learned more about writing from Hallie Ephron, Hank Phillippi Ryan, Kate Flora, and so many other sisters than I thought possible, and I have had such fun doing it.

I appreciate the loving encouragement and patience from my family and friends, including my biggest fan, Steve Dorsey, who has always believed in me more than I have myself.

My inspiration, the beautiful island and the wonderful people of St. John in the United States Virgin Islands, will always be in my heart and soul. I share their commitment to preserving St. John as the great jewel of the Caribbean. I am thankful to Mary-Phyllis Nogueira and Mary-Eileen Haim at Private Homes for Private Vacations for their gracious hospitality in St. John for more than thirty years.

So many of us enjoy reading a good mystery. It seems important to acknowledge that a fictional murder is far different from the senseless tragedy of a real one. The unsolved murder of Jimmy Malfetti in St. John in 2013 remains painfully real to his family and friends, who still seek justice and closure (http://www.justiceforjimmymalfetti.com).